**"We can take this as slowly as you want,"
Dom murmured.**

Sara glanced down at his aroused body as they
sprawled across his bed. "Uh, it looks like slow is
the last thing you need."

"I'll be fine." Dom smiled. When he kissed her, it
was gentle. Sweet. She'd wanted things to be wild,
untamed. This fantasy was turning into a soap
opera.

His hand cupped the back of her neck, and with the
tip of his tongue he brushed the seam between her
lips. His other hand caressed her breast and teased
the nipple.

Something clicked and she kissed him back, letting
everything else go. Right this moment, this kiss, his
tongue, the taste of him, the way he breathed, was
all that existed.

He didn't hurry her or make her feel anything but
special. His low moan made that thrill slip down her
back again, and she found herself melting inside, all
kinds of sensations wakening once more.

He wasn't the boy of her memories, or the man
she'd imagined.

He was so much better. Hotter. Sexier...

Dear Reader,

Well, here it is. My last Harlequin Blaze. It seems impossible. I've loved this series ever since I wrote my first Blaze back in 2001. I was thrilled that my editor, Birgit Davis-Todd, thought of me for the launch, and I've been privileged to write thirty-seven Blaze stories since then.

Seduced in the City is set in my beloved New York and is the final book in the NYC Bachelors trilogy.

Dominic Paladino is a natural-born charmer, and now that he's finally leaving the family business, everyone knows he's destined to take the world by storm.

Sara Moretti has returned to the neighborhood after being away at college, and is working at her family's pizza parlor while she finishes her MA. She'd had a crush on Dom since she was twelve.

Only, the boy she'd loved from afar broke her teenage heart, and she made a foolish mistake in return. Foolish enough that it rippled through her life right up until the day he reappeared ten years later.

Now they not only need to work through their troubled past, but they're faced with some serious decisions that could impact their families, their neighborhood and most important, the love that's taken them both by surprise.

I hope you enjoy Dom and Sara's story, and that we meet again soon between the pages of more stories from the heart.

All my best wishes,

Jo Leigh

Jo Leigh

Seduced in the City

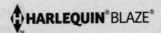

HARLEQUIN® BLAZE®

Recycling programs
for this product may
not exist in your area.

ISBN-13: 978-0-373-79962-6

Seduced in the City

Copyright © 2017 by Jolie Kramer

Printed in U.S.A.

www.Harlequin.com

A12006 902712

Jo Leigh is from Los Angeles and always thought she'd end up living in Manhattan. So how did she end up in Utah in a tiny town with a terrible internet connection, being bossed around by a houseful of rescued cats and dogs? What the heck, she says, predictability is boring. Jo has written more than sixty novels for Harlequin. Find her on Twitter, @jo_leigh.

To get the inside scoop on Harlequin Blaze and its talented writers, visit Facebook.com/BlazeAuthors.

All backlist available in ebook format.

Visit the Author Profile page at Harlequin.com for more titles.

To Birgit Davis-Todd, who's believed in me and my work since 1997.

I can't think of a better thing that's happened to me in my Harlequin career.

1

ELLIE, SARA MORETTI's little sister, hung up the phone and twirled around as if she'd just won the lottery. "The Paladinos want their regular order," she called back into the kitchen. "Two large, one pepperoni, one veggie, one order of ziti." She turned to Sara, her smile so broad it must have hurt. "I think Dom's coming to pick it up."

Dom.

The tray slipped out of Sara's hands and bounced on the linoleum floor with a loud clang.

Laughing, Ellie scooped it up for her. "Butterfingers."

Jeanette stuck her head out from the kitchen. "Everyone okay?"

"Fine." Sara took the tray from her sister and went straight to the sink to wash it.

She hadn't thought about Dominic Paladino in a long while. And clearly she couldn't afford to think about him now. Her pulse had ratcheted up. Her heart was trying out for the gymnastics team, and so was her stomach.

The last time she'd seen him was right there at Moretti's Pizza Parlor the day before she'd left for George Washington University, seven years ago. He'd been sitting at a table with two of his jock friends, his dark hair slicked back, his damp T-shirt straining across his broad shoulders and clinging to his lightly muscled chest. They'd just come from a soccer game after trampling their opponents, a team from the next block over. Sara had hid in the back while Jeanette waited on their table.

She glanced around, wondering what Ellie was up to. Was she staring? Had she already moved on? Of course she had. To her, Sara had dropped a tray. That's all. Ellie didn't know about Sara's long-ago crush on Dom, or what he'd said to shatter her young heart into a million pieces. No one had known about any of it because Sara had kept it to herself. Sort of… Years later she'd let her temper get the better of her and made a mistake that had cost her more than she could've imagined.

Ellie was checking on her table and laughing with the customers, so Sara relaxed. The place had barely changed. The old redbrick walls still looked as if they'd been put together by a bunch of drunks, the family-style tables still had red-checkered cloths, although she'd hoped they'd been replaced.

But it was home, and although she'd made more money serving cocktails in Washington, DC, in one night than she'd make here in a week, she was glad to be back in Little Italy.

"Bet you're surprised Dom is still here," Jeanette said from behind her.

"I hadn't really thought about it." She shrugged. "I guess I figured he'd be living out in Hollywood or someplace."

"Nah," Jeannette said, staring at the tray. Probably wondering if Sara had washed the aluminum off by now. The woman wasn't related by blood, but she'd been working there for over twenty years, so she was practically a Moretti. "The whole family's been sticking close to home since the old man had a second heart attack."

"Second? Oh, that's too bad," Sara said, meaning it. She'd known the Paladinos since she was a little kid. Her mom and Dom's mom had been friends since childhood, but Sara mostly knew them from church.

Jeanette smiled. "Joe's a tough old bird."

"I'm surprised my mom didn't mention it."

Jeanette took the tray to dry it. In a hushed voice she asked, "If Dom comes in, are you gonna hide in the back?"

Sara looked at her and laughed. "I was a shy nerd back then. Let him try pissing me off now."

Jeanette chuckled. "I might pay to see that."

"Who are you talking about?" Ellie popped up out of nowhere.

"No one you know," Sara said, drying her hands.

"Bet I do."

"Then let me rephrase. None of your business."

Jeanette grinned and shook her head.

Ellie huffed, grabbed some napkins and went back to her table.

Up until ninth grade Sara had gone to an all-girls Catholic school and hadn't seen much of Dom. But that had in no way stopped her from having a major crush on him, just like most of the girls in her class. Hell, the whole school. Every guy had wanted to be Dom, and all the girls had wanted him.

"His brother Tony's getting married," Ellie said, joining them behind the counter again.

"Whose brother?"

"Excuse me, ladies," Jeanette said with a little smile. "Gotta go back to the kitchen before Carlo starts yelling."

"Dom." Ellie stared at Sara as if she'd finally lost her last brain cell.

"Oh, of course. Silly me."

Ellie ignored the sarcasm. "I wonder if Dom is going to be the best man. Can you imagine him in a tux?"

"Oh, sweetie," Sara said, not surprised, really. "Tell me you don't have a thing for that guy. For God's sake, he's a year older than me, and you think I'm the Crypt Keeper."

"You're almost thirty." Lifting her chin, Ellie left to go wipe down table five, where a gang of slobs, also known as high school kids, had left their mark everywhere from the tablecloth to the floor.

"I'm twenty-seven, thank you. But I believe I've made my point."

Ellie sighed. "Have you met any seventeen-year-old boys? They're disgusting."

"You think that changes when they turn twenty-eight?"

"He's hot. And he doesn't look old." Ellie's cheeks got splotchy. Poor kid had a blush like a rash. Although she was so pretty it didn't really make a difference. With her waist-length brown hair and her big green eyes, she was the beauty of the family.

Sara had been the brainy one, but all that had gotten her was an almost-completed master's degree and a load of student debt.

"So, I assume he's still single?" Sara said, and got another funny look from Ellie. "Since you're shamelessly mooning over him."

Her sister broke out in laughter. "Mooning? Jeez, Sara, you sound like Nonna."

Sara came out from behind the counter and snatched a pair of salt-and-pepper shakers that needed refilling. "Don't change the subject."

"What, like you did when I asked about you and Robert?"

"Oh, my God. Why did I come back here?" Sara heard a call from the kitchen and she went to get the order ready for the Cho family. Chinatown pretty much surrounded Little Italy now. Most of their customers lived there, or in Nolita or SoHo. At least people still kept coming to their place, even if they had other pizza joints closer. Thank goodness they kept getting those "Best in New York" awards.

Not that they were making a lot of money. Enough to keep up with the cost of living, but that was about it. Fortunately, their rent was still amazingly cheap, so they weren't about to make any changes. What would her parents do if they didn't run this place? As the sign above the marquee proudly proclaimed, Moretti's had been in the family since 1931.

She thought about Robert as she sliced the large Sicilian pie, then closed the box. He'd been in Rome for two months now, and while they talked two or three times a week, she wasn't quite sure where that left their relationship. For the three years she'd known Robert, he'd wanted to work for *Inside the Vatican*. More than he wanted anything, including her. Oh, he'd argue otherwise, but she knew better.

There were two salads to go, which she put in the cold bag, along with the liter of soda. Then she stuck it all on the pickup counter and turned to the next pizza while Jeannette caught another phone order. The dinner hour had just begun and they were already slammed. Especially with that birthday party for twelve coming up.

The bell above the door rang, but instead of Mike Cho, it was Dominic who walked into the restaurant.

Sara stilled, and in the span of a second she was thirteen years old again, a geeky, flat-chested, mousy little girl who'd cried for two whole nights, convinced her life was over.

He'd changed. Broader chest, a hint of a five o'clock shadow on his strong jaw, his swagger more assured. He'd been the best-looking guy in school, but now he might just be the best-looking guy in New York. His eyes seemed darker, and his hair looked like her fingers would get lost in those thick brown waves, and for heaven's sake, even his smile had gotten more charming.

As if she didn't dislike him enough already.

But it certainly made sense that Ellie had a crush on him. One quick glance at Jeannette, and yep, she wasn't immune either. Sara remembered how she'd written *Mrs. Dominic Paladino, Mrs. Sara Paladino and Mrs. Sarafina Paladino* ad nauseum on a half dozen notebooks starting at age twelve. Which stopped abruptly at age thirteen, after *that day*. She'd destroyed notebooks, journal entries, anything that mentioned him, purging him from her life.

The next year it was time to make the big switch to high school. Even though she'd begged her parents to let her go to the all-girls Catholic school in Midtown, they'd sent her to Loyola. The school ruled by Dom and all his jock friends.

Lucky for her, he'd barely acknowledged that she was alive.

At least now she could return the favor.

Dom Paladino had been grateful to get out of his folks' house for a little while. The conversation had turned to Tony's wedding. Again. Even with Catherine's parents all the way in Europe, everyone, including them, felt compelled to throw in their two cents.

Poor Catherine had been getting it from both sides. She was trying her best to keep the affair to a manageable size but her folks—both diplomats who had about a million political "friends" that *had* to be invited—didn't seem to know the meaning of compromise. At this rate, they'd have to get St. Patrick's Cathedral to hold them all. Dom had told Tony to elope a dozen times, but had his eldest brother listened? Fine. His business, his problem. Just as Dom had left the house, the discussion had turned to the relatives who still lived in Italy that should be on the guest—

His thoughts skidded to a halt. Was that Sara?

Holy shit, she'd...blossomed.

He greeted Ellie and Jeannette in his usual manner, but his gaze was magnetically drawn to Sara Moretti. He hadn't seen her in years and damn, she looked hot. Gorgeous light brown hair that hit just below her shoulders. And those eyes of hers. If he'd had any doubt she was Sara, those big hazel eyes would've confirmed it. He tried to imagine that skinny, shy kid with braces from his past, but her transformation was too impressive. Probably still smart as could be, though. "Sara?"

She gave him an abrupt nod, then turned her back to slice a large pizza.

Above the piped-in Italian music, he heard Ellie gasp.

He didn't get it. Why had Sara been so curt? He tried to remember if he'd done anything bad to her back in the day. He didn't think so. Yeah, at times he'd been an arrogant little shit in high school, but not usually. Mostly out of rebellion, considering he had his older brothers' reputations to live up to.

Dom honestly couldn't remember having much interaction with Sara, not even at church functions or here in her family's pizza parlor.

"How are the wedding plans coming along?" Ellie asked.

"Oh, man. I don't want to even hear the word *wedding*. The whole thing is insane. If I ever start talking about that, remind me, would you?"

"I bet Tony's excited." Ellie blushed as she went over to the soda machine. She poured him a cola, squeezed a piece of lime, put a lid on it, slid in a straw and handed the cup to Dom. "Here you go."

"Thanks, Ellie. The boys at school still driving you crazy? Say the word and I'll make sure they behave."

"Stop it," she said, the pink on her cheeks looking a little spotted. "They're all stupid."

"Still no one special then?"

"Ew, no."

He laughed, just as Mike Cho, a guy he knew from Loyola, then the local gym, came into the restaurant.

"Dominic," Mike said. "What's the matter? You don't lift anymore?"

"I moved. I'm living in the Cast Iron District now."

"That's not far."

"No," Dom said. "But I've been going to Body Space Fitness in Union Square."

"I heard that's a good place. They have a pool, right?"

"And killer instructors."

"Can you hook me up with a pass? I might be willing to take the bus for a pool."

"Sure. I'll give you a call."

Sara came to the counter, carrying a big take-out bag for Mike along with his pizza. "That'll be twenty-six fifty."

"You new here?" Mike asked, his voice dropping half an octave as he forgot that her eyes were above her chest.

"That's Sara Moretti," Dom said. "She's been away at college. Studying…journalism?"

Sara glanced at him as if she hadn't realized he could speak full sentences. "That's right." Then she looked at Mike again. "I remember you from Loyola. You wrote for the paper a couple of times."

"You're that Sara? Wow. You've changed."

"I hope so." Sara smiled. "It's good to see you again."

"Yeah, same here. How long have you been back?"

"Just a week."

"So, you here to stay?" Mike asked.

"I'm not sure," she said with a small shrug that drew Dom's attention to her breasts straining the fabric of her T-shirt. "I'm working on my master's thesis so I'll be here long enough to finish it."

Dom realized he was behaving as badly as Mike had, and he snapped his attention up to her face. Her lips were moving but Dom hadn't heard a thing she'd said.

She and Mike laughed about something, and then Sara asked, "Will that be cash?"

Cho whipped out his wallet, fumbled with his credit card, then smiled at her with such eagerness, Dom debated getting him that gym pass.

While Sara swiped Mike's card, he looked at Dom, lifting his brows in what was supposed to be a guy-bonding moment. Dom ignored it. He wasn't sure why he was irritable. Mike was a good guy. They'd competed in track.

As Sara handed him back his card, Mike grinned. "You made that paper a decent read," he said. "Much better than Billy Calabrini."

"Thanks. That's nice of you, but if you'll excuse me. I have to—" She nodded her chin in the direction of the kitchen and drifted toward the prep counter.

Mike's grin faded with every step she took. But that didn't stop him from eyeing how those worn jeans cupped her ass. "Well, can't win 'em all," he said. He turned for the door. "Later."

"Yeah, later." Of course Dom had been checking her out also. But that was different. He took a sip of his soda, then got out his wallet when he saw Sara packing up his order. He put cash on the counter, then a tip in the jar. Like always. When she came with his stuff, he smiled—

not as enthusiastically as Mike had. "You never asked me to write for the paper."

"Mike volunteered," she said, not meeting his gaze.

"I didn't know that was an option."

"It was," she said, as she stared at his soda. A moment later, he watched her add the cost to his bill before she rang it up. "Besides, as I recall, you were always too busy."

"Uh-oh. I think I must have done something to you back in school."

She didn't answer at first, just stared down. "What do you mean?"

"Charging for the soda?" he said, joking. Trying to get her to lighten up. Maybe she'd caught him checking her out and was pissed. "I mean, I'm happy to pay for it, but…"

Ellie rushed over to her sister's side and bumped Sara's shoulder. "I'm sure you never did anything bad to her. She's just been gone too long and doesn't know the routine anymore."

Dom smiled, trying to figure out the expression on Sara's face. Was she really annoyed about the buck seventy-five, or was this about something else? He hadn't seen Sara in years and—

Jesus. The long-ago memory flashed like lightning through his brain. How could he have forgotten? This wasn't about anything Dom had done to her. It had been the other way around. As the editor of the school paper, Sara had practically eviscerated him in an op-ed piece, and he'd never been more insulted in his entire life.

"I know the routine," Sara told her sister. "I've worked here more years than you."

"Sara," Ellie said, her voice a little condescending. "Not now, okay?"

Sara glared at her. "I don't remember Dad saying anything ever about giving out freebies. And surely Mr. Hot-shot can afford to pay for it."

Ellie, looking shocked and embarrassed, cleared her throat. "I'll just charge the order to your family account, okay?" Then she spun around on Sara and in a hushed voice muttered, "What is your problem?"

Dom could still hear, though, and clearly this was the perfect opening. He could've taken the high road—after all, they'd been kids. But with her acting like this? "Ellie, why don't you ask Sara about the article she wrote my last year at Loyola?" he said, gathering his order and holding Sara's gaze captive.

She should've looked embarrassed. Maybe even blushed. Not look as if she wanted to give him a third nostril.

"Yeah?" she said with an accusing smile. "And ask Dom what he said about—" She stopped short and blinked. "Never mind."

"Go ahead," he said, honestly drawing a blank. "About what? I'd like to hear this."

Her inhale was sharp, and her cheeks flushed dark pink. Without a word she turned around and disappeared into the kitchen.

2

"Um, sorry, Dom," Ellie said, "Sara's...she's, uh, been kind of crazy working on her thesis. Lots of late nights and all. So, uh, she probably didn't mean anything."

Sara listened from behind the wall separating the kitchen from the front counter area. God, what a coward, letting her kid sister take the heat. Although she hadn't asked Ellie to make excuses for her.

"Yeah, I'm sure she didn't," Dom said. "See you later, Ellie."

Sara took a quick peek and watched him balance the container of ziti on the two pizza boxes. As soon as he paused and turned his head toward the kitchen, she ducked back out of sight.

"I'll get the door for you," Ellie said, and hurried out from behind the counter.

Waiting until she heard the bell over the door, Sara closed her eyes, grateful Dom was gone. Of course he'd remembered what she had written about him. But why she'd risen to the bait in such a humiliating way made her sick. She should have just ignored him, pretended she didn't know what he was talking about. It had happened ten years ago. He wouldn't have pursued the topic. He would've just left, and she'd still have a little dignity.

"What the heck was that about?" Ellie asked, her voice so indignant it made Sara jerk back to look at her.

"Why did you give him the free soda?" Sara brushed past her, remembering at the last second to grab a clean rag, as if anyone would believe she'd disappeared for any reason but the obvious.

"We never charge him."

"You're joking, right? Is this just for Dom, or for every guy you have a crush on?"

"It has nothing to do with me having a crush on him. And who says I do, anyway?"

Sara rolled her eyes and put some elbow grease into wiping off the tables.

"I only give free soda to Dom," Ellie said, glaring, her face blotchy. "Jeannette does it, too. So do the others."

"For God's sake, why?" Sara stopped and glared back. "Because he's hot?"

"I—we—give him free sodas because he's a very good customer."

"We have a lot of good customers. I can't believe you just give him free stuff. What's next? Pizzas on the house because his smile is pearly white?"

Ellie's hands went to her hips, and she gave Sara a look that reminded her of how they used to argue over their single bathroom sink. "Because he always leaves good tips."

"Enough to make up for the loss in soda?"

"Why don't you take a look, smart-ass?"

That was new.

Ellie got the tip jar and pulled out a twenty. "This is what he leaves for a big order. For a slice, he leaves five dollars. Minimum. Every time."

Sara knew what the markup was on soda. And leaving

that kind of tip each time he came in actually did make up for those freebies, and then some. She hadn't expected that. "Okay, so he likes playing big shot and throwing his money around. Fine. Let him."

Ellie kept staring. "I can't believe how horrible you were to him. What did you write in the paper?"

"Nothing. We were kids. Look, I lost my temper. I'm tired and I saw you treating him like he was king of the neighborhood, and it pissed me off, okay?" Sara had regretted the big shot remark—and just about everything else—even before she saw the disappointment in her sister's eyes. "I'm sorry, El. It won't happen again. I promise."

Ellie gave her a halfhearted nod. Probably more than Sara deserved, so she smiled back.

The bell over the door rang twice, and they both got to work greeting customers and handing out menus. Hopefully, the place would be so busy with that big party it would let her forget what had happened. With any luck, which seemed to be in short supply for her lately, she'd scared Dom off from ever coming to Moretti's again.

But this was Little Italy. If she really thought she wouldn't see him again, and soon, she was dreaming.

On Thursday, after Dominic had finished putting in the data for Paladino & Sons' newest customers, he hurried to the printers, where he went through each page of the new restoration brochure he'd had printed. He'd spent a lot of time designing it using photographs he'd taken of different houses and buildings they'd restored. The centerpiece was Catherine's remodeled single-family home, its 1930s art deco glory brought to life with amazing results.

He'd worked even harder on the copy, so when he got to the last fold and saw that his description of the revitalized fireplace tiles had been shortened, he wasn't pleased.

"Kenny. What happened here?"

"What's that?" The owner of the printing press that Dom had been using for the last five years read the paragraph in question. "Ah, the Verdana font you asked for wouldn't fit completely on the page, so I nipped that one sentence a little."

"Why didn't you call me?"

Ken Patterson, who was about twenty years older than Dom, seemed startled by his tone. "It was just a few words, and I know you wanted that particular font."

Dom liked the guy. He'd always done a great job at a good price on time. "I'm sorry, buddy, but in this case, it's not going to work out. I want it printed again, only this time use Helvetica. The sentence you abbreviated targets a particular market, which I wouldn't expect you to know. But in the future, call me, all right?"

Kenny nodded, his relief obvious. "Sure thing, Dom. I'll turn these around real quick. How's Monday afternoon?"

"Great." He held out his hand, and they shook. Dom felt certain a mistake like that wouldn't happen again.

Then he was off to an interview for a position at *New York Adventures*, a web and subscription magazine. He probably didn't have much chance of getting it, but what the hell. Now that he was finished with his graduate studies, the job hunt was on.

For now, though, he was busier than ever with the family construction business, what with Tony tasting wedding cake samples and checking out reception venues, and Luca being so in demand as a finish carpenter that he'd accrued quite a list of private clients.

Dom was glad for his brothers. They'd busted their asses when their dad had gotten sick. It was time the little brother stepped up, gave them some breathing room. And with the business growing in different directions, he was actually learning new things along the way. Sure, he wanted to do much more careerwise, but for now, this was fine.

Several hours later he had to remind himself that life was good.

Yeah, for some other guy, maybe.

It had turned into one of those days. Everything had taken longer than it should have. And he didn't know where the hell all the cabs in the city had disappeared to, only that he'd waited three times for more than ten minutes. Which gave him far too much headspace to think about Sara Moretti.

In those snug jeans and stretchy blue top.

Holy shit, she might've been a late bloomer, if memory served, but nature had made it up to her in a big way.

Since seeing her the other evening, his brain had been stuck in a damn loop. First, the jeans and clingy top. Next came the memory of those almond-shaped hazel eyes that could make a man forget his own name. And finally the thing that nagged him the most—the great mystery. Sara believed he'd wronged her in some way, and for the life of him he couldn't figure out what he'd done.

He'd been thinking about it far too often. And he'd come up with the same conclusion each time. She must've mixed him up with someone else. It was the only thing that made sense because he'd barely said a dozen words to her the three years they'd attended the same school.

Only one thing to do about it. He had to ask her what it was she thought she remembered. She'd try to ignore him, or tell him she was joking, and normally he'd let it go. In fact, he would've preferred to forget she'd said anything. But the damn thought had popped up right in the middle of his interview.

For a few seconds it had thrown him off track. Thankfully, he'd recovered quickly and he'd gotten a good vibe from the woman, but he wasn't going to let himself get excited. The job was technically for someone with more experience. If that was the case, fine. At least it had been good practice. But being distracted by thoughts of Sara's imaginary slight? He couldn't have that.

He'd ask her what she meant, and he wouldn't leave without an answer. The question was should he go to Moretti's now? He was tired and he still needed to hit the gym.

Dom stuck his hand out for a taxi that zipped right past him. Perfect. He glanced at his watch. They'd be closing real soon. Probably a good time to catch her. If she wanted to lock up, she'd have to answer him first.

A FAMILY OF four were the only customers left in the restaurant at eight minutes to closing. As if any of them cared about that. A minute ago the older teen tried to order a custom pizza to go. Sara didn't bother asking Carlo if he had time—he would've bitten her head off. If they'd been regulars she would've considered it. But she was fairly certain they were tourists.

She kept on wiping down tables while Carlo was wrapping up in the kitchen. The day had been particularly busy. The dining room floor needed a washing, but Carlo would do that, which was why he was anxious to close. As soon as table three paid, she'd start cashing out.

A long night at her laptop awaited her, and she doubted she'd get home before ten. She didn't really mind because she was excited about finally getting started on her thesis. This morning she'd begun the lengthy interview process by meeting with her first subjects, Mr. and Mrs. Scarpetti. The couple currently lived in Brooklyn, but their families had come over in 1880 from Napoli, and Mr. Scarpetti remembered a lot of stories from the very early days. Some from when the Five Points area had been the nexus of what had been called the worst slum in the United States.

Despite the realities of living in squalor, sweet memories always bled through the tragedies. That was one of the reasons she'd made "The History of Little Italy, 1810-1940," her thesis. Her focus was on collecting stories from families who'd been there since the early days, like hers, and comparing them to historical records. Giving their local history a face and name.

She'd wanted to transcribe the complete Scarpetti tapes tonight, but they'd talked for a long time. It would take her hours, and she wasn't sure she had it in her.

When the bell rang over the door, Sara turned, ready to send away whoever was coming in this late. But once again, she was stopped in her tracks by Dominic.

So much for scaring him off.

It had been only three days since she'd seen him, but he looked like a different guy. Disheveled, hair sticking up oddly, his necktie askew, as if he'd come though a wind tunnel. When he caught sight of her, he ran a hand through his hair, although it didn't do much good.

She acknowledged him with a brief smile. Only because he'd seen her look up. Then wondered about her own hair after hustling all day. She almost smoothed it back but caught herself. He was still staring directly at her when she lowered her gaze to the table she must've wiped down a hundred times already. A dozen more swipes couldn't hurt.

It took him all of three seconds before he was standing across the table from her, though she refused to look up. "Are you alone?" he asked.

"Carlo's in the back." She had just enough sense to switch to another table, and then wiped it down for all she was worth, unsure what to say, and not wanting to look him in the eyes.

"Can I talk to you for a minute, Sara?"

"I'm the only one on the floor. Can't you see we're busy?"

He glanced around the nearly empty pizza parlor, amusement flickering on his face, but he wisely kept his mouth shut. "No problem. I'll wait."

Great. Maybe she should get it over with while she had witnesses.

"Look, I know it's a long shot," Dom said, "but I haven't eaten all day. Any chance you have a slice on hand?"

Out of the corner of her eye she saw the couple and their two kids getting to their feet. *Now* they cared about closing time? "A slice? This late? You know better than that."

"Yeah, I suppose I do."

"Anyway, Carlo closed the kitchen ten minutes ago."

"So, anything? A pizza someone didn't pick up?" Dom said. "I don't mind buying the whole pie."

His tie landed on the chair back. She blinked, but it was still there. "What are you doing?" she asked, shooting a gaze up at him.

"Sorry, sweetheart, not what you think," he said, loosening his collar and grinning. "Only on Friday and Saturday nights and I charge a cover."

"Why am I not surprised?" A sudden image of Dom, naked, lingered a moment too long and she felt the heat creeping up her throat. "Do you know how lucky you are there are customers here?"

"Believe me, I thought of that before I said anything."

"Excuse me," she murmured, dropping the rag on the table and squeezing past him. Dom might look the worse for wear, but he sure smelled good. Musky with a hint of spice. No cheap cologne for him.

Dad already had his money out. Mom was tucking a tip under her glass.

"How was everything?" Sara asked with a smile. "May I get you anything else?"

The couple exchanged looks and laughed.

"You mean I can I get that artichoke and shrimp pizza?" The older boy had made it to the door but turned back with a hopeful expression.

Sara wanted to jump off the nearest bridge.

"We don't have time, Dillon. We need to get back to the hotel and pack."

"Come on, Dad. Really?"

God only knew what it was in her expression that prompted his parents to come to her rescue, but she was grateful. Sara gave them an extra smile, wishing she could return their tip. "How would you like to take some tiramisu with you?" she asked. "On the house."

The teen frowned. "Tira-what?"

"No, thank you." The woman glanced briefly at Dom and smiled at Sara. "We're fine," she said, and shooed the rest of the family out the door.

Sara picked up the check and money they'd left on the table and took it to the register. "I think we have a Hawaiian in the cooler," she told Dom, and almost laughed at the face he made.

But it didn't stop him for a second. "I'll take it."

"Sit down." She walked into the kitchen, not the least bit pleased that even looking like he'd been through the ringer, he still made her insides quiver. She should have been over him years ago, the moment she'd overheard him talking to his friends about the dance, and yet there it was. That stupid little thrill. Just another one of the neighborhood girls who swooned the moment he showed up.

So embarrassing.

She got the pizza from the fridge, while he waited at the counter, turning over the take-out menu. As she got closer, his stomach rumbled so loudly she thought Carlo had probably heard. "You want me to heat a slice?"

"That would be fantastic."

"I'm talking about the microwave. We've already turned off the ovens."

"Microwave. Campfire. Cigarette lighter. It all works."

"Here," she said, handing him a medium drink cup. "Come on back and fix yourself a soda. You're going to have to eat fast, because seriously..."

"You're closing in three minutes." He took the cup and lifted the divider that kept the customers in their place. "You always work by yourself at night?"

She rounded the corner and popped his slice in the microwave. "No," she said, returning to the counter. "Jeanette left at eight."

"Where's your pop? I haven't seen him in a while."

"He took my mom to visit family in Sicily."

"Huh." Dom looked puzzled.

"What? Because he never takes a vacation?"

"Well, yeah, that, too. I'm just surprised there are any Italians left in Sicily. I heard it was being overrun by outsiders."

"You mean like Little Italy?"

"So, you noticed, huh?"

"Hard not to." Sara didn't mistake the easy small talk for a get-out-of-jail-free card. At any minute he was going to ask her what she'd meant the other night, and she didn't know what to tell him. A lie wasn't beneath her, if she was able to think up a good one. Just so she could put the whole stupid thing to rest.

A loud bang from the kitchen made her jump.

"Carlo, you okay?"

After a muttered string of curses in Italian, he said, "Yeah."

Sara and Dom exchanged smiles.

Even after her seven-year foray into the world beyond Little Italy, Dominic Paladino was still the best-looking man she'd ever seen. It didn't help that he was standing so close. She should've gotten his soda instead of inviting him into her space.

Dammit, the tummy fluttering had to stop. Now.

Dom was still looking directly at her. "So he'll walk you home?"

"Who?"

"Carlo."

"What are you talking about?" she asked as she made her break to the other side and went over to clear off the last dirty table. "Walk me home? I live five blocks from here."

"I know. But it's late."

"Nine o'clock is nothing. There's plenty of traffic. Some nights we let groups hold meetings here and I don't get out before eleven."

"What? That's crazy."

"Tell my dad that. He's the one that says it's our civic duty. Although how hosting a chess club is considered civic duty is beyond me." She didn't dare stop. If Dom knew he'd momentarily thrown her off balance, he didn't show it. She walked right past him, straight to the microwave in back. "Your slice should be ready."

Of course it wasn't hot because she hadn't set enough time. She added fifteen seconds and drummed her fingers on the counter while she waited, thankful for the partition between them. So far, so good, but she still hadn't come up with anything to say when he finally asked about the elephant in the room.

The microwave dinged.

Sara took a deep breath.

Dom was already on the other side of the counter, putting the top on his soda when she came around the wall.

"Here," she said, setting the paper plate in front of him. "If you want another slice you have to tell me now, because—"

"You're leaving. No, thanks. One will get me home fine." His smile dazzled, as always, but he looked tired. Like he'd had a rough day.

She smiled back, wondering what had put the faint lines at the corners of his eyes. The tie and blazer probably meant he'd just gotten off work. Despite what she'd written in the article, she'd known he was a good student and a hard worker. "Look, Dom—"

"Sara—"

They spoke in unison. He motioned for her to go first. Nodding, she said, "I owe you a long-overdue apology."

3

DOM REMEMBERED THAT shy smile though he didn't know why he should. He hadn't really noticed her much back in school. And she wanted to apologize? He hadn't seen that coming.

Earlier, when they'd been talking about the old neighborhood, they'd had a moment where they'd connected. The past had briefly converged with the present. And then something had happened, but he didn't know what.

"I shouldn't have written that op-ed piece. It was wrong and I knew it and I still—"

"Hey, you don't need to do this," he said, cutting her short. "That's all in the past. We were kids. I shouldn't have brought it up. Wait." He thought for a moment. "Wrong to write the article or wrong because you knew it wasn't true?"

"Here," she said, pushing a bunch of napkins at him.

"You must think I'm a real slob." When he reached for one, his fingers brushed against hers. Something twitched, nothing big. A reminder that he was aware of how soft her skin looked, of the way her hips flared. How the shirt clung to her breasts.

"I don't want to see you get sauce on that snazzy blazer."

He glanced down and shrugged. "I had to meet with two new clients, and then I had an interview."

Behind him, the bell over the door rang.

Sara tilted her head to the side to see who it was. "Sorry, we're closed," she said with a warm smile she had yet to give him. Although he kind of liked that little shy one. "Come back tomorrow. We're open at ten."

After some grumbling, the door closed.

"I need to go lock up."

"Okay, I get the hint."

"No, I wasn't—" She almost touched his hand but stopped herself and grabbed a ring of keys. "No rush. At least for the next ten minutes."

Dom stripped the offensive pineapple off his pizza and took a bite as he watched her walk to the door. Those jeans couldn't have fit her any better. He wondered if she knew she had *the perfect* ass.

While she fiddled with getting the key in the lock, he quickly took two more bites, just to get his stomach to shut up. When Sara turned to make the return trip, he whipped out his wallet and pretended he hadn't been checking her out.

"How much do I owe you?"

"Don't worry about it. I was going to keep that one in the fridge so we could give out slices tomorrow for our homeless regulars."

"What happened to no free food, ever?"

Her eyebrows went up, and he laughed.

"I didn't know you guys did that. That's great." He pulled out a twenty and slid it over to her.

"I know. I'm proud of my folks." She frowned at the money. "I just told you—"

"Consider that my contribution to the program."

She sighed. "Obviously I can't say no to that. Thank

you," she said, picking up the twenty and going to the register. She put it in an envelope way in the back of the drawer, then took out a stack of bills.

"Am I in the way?" He realized he should've moved to a table. They had more talking to do and he had a feeling she'd be less open with him right there in her face.

"You're fine," she said just as he picked up his plate and moved.

He glanced over at Sara and caught her looking back, and she might've been checking him out, too. And here he was in conservative gray dress slacks. *Shit.*

"Hey, I heard about your father's heart attack. How's he doing?"

He quickly swallowed. "Good. Retired. Not liking it much. But his health is better."

"Good. And Tony, he's—" Sara lifted a brow. "Is 'getting married' okay, or does it fall in the banned words category?"

"I'll make an exception," he said. "Yeah, Tony's getting married. Catherine's great. They're good together."

"I'm happy for them."

"You know Tony?"

She finished counting her stack before she shoved it in a bank bag. "Not really. I don't think we ever said so much as hi." She shrugged. "Kind of like how I know you."

If she didn't know Tony, then basically she was running out the clock. Too bad. He still had a question for her.

"Did you ever go to college?" she asked, searching around the register, lifting receipts, moving the pizza box.

"More than I ever thought I would. Two masters, can you believe it?"

She touched her hair and sighed as she pulled the pencil from behind her ear. "Yeah, that makes sense. For a jock you were no slouch in the grades department."

Dom knew the exact moment she realized what she'd said. Her eyes widened for a split second and she looked down, gaze glued to the stack in front of her. Well, that was one question answered. She'd known it was bullshit, but she'd printed it anyway. Still curious as hell, he pretended he hadn't noticed the slip and took another bite. Chewed. Then said, "I wasn't a jock."

"All the different sports you played? Of course you were."

"That's not all I did." Damn, he was getting tired of people homing in on superficial qualities. He had the ambition and smarts to do lots of things with his life.

"It's not like being a jock was bad. That wasn't what I meant."

"Hey, I just thought of something…about you," he said, and grinned at the dread on her face. "You kicking ass and taking names when you were editor of the paper. Christ, that one day you were riled up about cafeteria lunches and the faculty doing something stupid. We were all packed into the gym for some announcement." He took a sip of his soda, his memory suddenly clear as a photograph. "You wore that pink sweater, the one with the cats on it."

She gave him a one-sided grin. "You remember that?"

"You rained down hell on the entire staff. I always wondered if your grades tanked after that."

The grin was faint but still there, and now her head tilted slightly to the left. "Huh." She picked up another stack of bills.

"I graduated a few months later. I assume you were editor your senior year."

Sara's smile vanished and she looked down at her hands. Guess he'd assumed wrong. He wondered what had done her in, giving it to the faculty or writing a slanderous implication about him. He'd been plenty pissed, but he hadn't said anything, not to anyone who mattered. Just his friends and Coach Randal. Pissed on his behalf, they'd urged him to file a complaint but he hadn't.

"I think the emergency has passed," he said, although he was still hungry. They'd been talking. Everything was good. But he'd lost ground with her. "Why don't you put the rest of the pizza back in the fridge, give it to your regulars tomorrow?"

He stood up and had the unexpected pleasure of watching her walk to the fridge. Not on purpose but he couldn't have timed it better. "You going home soon?"

She didn't respond at first. "About ten minutes."

"I'll stick around and walk with you." He wasn't surprised by her hesitation. "You know this neighborhood isn't what it used to be."

"Dom. It's still practically rush hour out there. Go home. I'll even refill your soda."

"I'm good." He stood as he watched her count another stack of bills, pretty sure her deep concentration had more to do with ignoring him. He just didn't know why.

"Hey, Dom. I thought that was your voice." Carlo, one of the nicest guys in the neighborhood—even though he looked like he'd beat you up just for breathing—came from the back, his forehead beaded with perspiration. "Can you guys take this outside? I gotta wash the floor."

"Dom was just leaving," Sara said, and grabbed the keys. "I'm still cashing out."

He studied her flushed face for a moment as Carlo started turning chairs upside down on the tables. Sara stubbornly refused to meet his eyes. "See you, Carlo," Dom said on his way to the door, then gave her one last look before he opened the door and stepped outside. He heard the lock click behind him.

Yeah, well the hell with that. She couldn't lock him out forever. No, he'd get his answer, one way or another.

IT TOOK A lot longer than ten minutes for Sara to leave. She said goodnight to Carlo, who stopped mopping to let her out. Poor guy would be at it for another hour. She'd been working since early that morning, making the weekly run to Costco to pick up staples for the restaurant and for the family, before meeting with the Scarpettis. But now, even the idea of listening to the soft, crackly voice of Mr. Scarpetti made her wish she'd majored in math.

It had been a good day, though. Ellie had been in a decent mood when she'd worked the early shift, and they'd made excellent tips. Lots of American tourists and regulars.

Then there was Dom.

It had been nice for a while. She'd realigned her opinion of him, and he'd proved again that he could be generous. That she'd dodged his question didn't mean he was going quietly into the night. She was already regretting that she hadn't taken advantage of the rare privacy to make sure everything stayed in the past where it belonged.

He'd given her an opening. He'd been willing to forgive and forget, chalk up the article to stupid kid stuff. She should've leaped onto that and admitted she'd been a silly, hormonal teenager, lied and said he hadn't really done anything bad and could they just move on.

The offer to walk her home had been a nice touch. Misguided, but sweet. She'd like to think he'd do that for any of the girls who had to clock out late. In fact, she planned to ask Ellie about that in the morning.

But tonight, she'd stop thinking anything about Dominic, nice or not, and gear herself up for her thesis work.

Maybe.

No. She could manage an hour. As long as she had her feet up and Ellie left her alone. Sara would be crazy not to make use of the time with her folks away. She loved them dearly, but her parents had never run across a closed door they didn't feel free to open. She could lock them out, but she wouldn't. She hadn't been home long enough. Soon, though, they'd get back to how it had been.

She crossed the street, her hand on her purse, which was slung cross-body style. As if she didn't know how to handle herself in this neighborhood. Of course her sneaky thoughts had slid back to Dom.

Ten minutes later she was home but it took her another thirty to unwind, to get Dom Paladino out of her head, to quiet thoughts of the cataclysmic fallout that his formal complaint to the school board had caused. It actually hadn't mattered if he'd heard the whole story, or that he hadn't expressed any regret for taking his complaint to the extreme. She'd needed to apologize for her part. To own her mistake.

But that minor revelation had only come after she'd straightened her desk, adjusted her chair, made the perfect pot of tea and started transcribing the first interview tape.

Mr. Scarpetti's voice tended to weaken at the end of his sentences, and Mrs. Scarpetti had a unique Italian accent, so Sara had to do a lot of rewinding to get the full meaning of most of their stories.

But finally, by eleven, she'd gotten accustomed to the voices and the work started to flow.

Which was precisely the moment Ellie barged into Sara's bedroom. Barged, as in bounced the doorknob off the wall as she entered.

Sara jumped, knocked her recorder to the floor, and spun around prepared to meet a knife-wielding man wearing a balaclava. "What the hell are you doing?"

"Sorry," Ellie lied. "I forgot this door is so loose. Listen, I've got—"

"I don't care what you've got. You knock before you come into this room. I'm working here, not painting my nails. It's going to take me forever to get back into the transcription, especially since you scared the crap out of me."

Ellie seemed shocked. She'd been home studying and was wearing a Lemonade sleep shirt. With no makeup on, her blinking seemed a little understated. "You really think people in this house are going to knock on your door?"

Closing her eyes didn't help Sara calm down at all, nor did the truth of Ellie's statement. "I'll take steps."

"They won't let you get a lock."

"They won't have a choice. Although I'm kind of amazed they left so much of my stuff here. I had no idea I'd ever be back."

"Mom never believed anything else."

Sara sighed. "So you've got…"

"A thing on Thursday. It's going to run late. Just letting you know."

"A bank robbery? Broadway tickets?"

"Very funny. Shopping for a prom dress. With Tina."

At least Sara knew who Tina was. "So, Mom would be okay with you going out on a school night?"

Ellie pressed her lips together for a moment, before letting out a breath. "I'm allowed on special occasions."

"What's wrong with the weekend?"

"Tina knows someone at Sak's Off 5th and she's going to let us use her employee discount. But the only night her friend works is Thursday."

"Okay," Sara said. "But why would you be late?"

"We have to be there at the end of the night. They close at ten."

"What time is your regular curfew?"

"God." Ellie rolled her eyes. "I'm seventeen. Not twelve."

Sara gave her a stare only a sister could deliver.

"Okay. Fine. It's midnight."

"On a weeknight? Really?"

Thinking back to when she was a teenager living under the draconian rules of her old-fashioned parents, she had some sympathy for Ellie. Although Sara hadn't needed a prom dress because she hadn't gone, she'd secretly been heartbroken over her lack of a date. And she hadn't had to deal with an older sister either. Maybe this would be a good time to show a little solidarity.

"On weekdays it's ten," Ellie said, sighing loudly. "Come on, Sara… It's the *prom* and I don't have a dress yet."

"Wow, I hardly ever got to go out on a weeknight. And on weekends I had to be home by eleven."

"Well, that was before cell phones. Or cars."

"Ha. You're hilarious."

Grinning, Ellie ran her hand over the antique dresser that had once belonged to a second cousin. "Anyway, you owe me."

"What are you talking about?"

"The other night when you chased Dom away. Who knows when he'll come back? He'll probably find some other place to get his pizzas."

"That's absurd. He was just there."

That caught Ellie's attention more than anything Sara had said. "When?"

"Tonight. Right before closing." Sara lined up the pencils that had been jostled by Ellie's explosive entry.

Ellie looked positively crestfallen. "What did he want?"

"A slice."

"That late?"

"Exactly what I told him."

She studied Sara with an accusing glare, then spun around for the door.

Seventeen hadn't been that long ago for Sara and something twisted inside her. "Ellie?"

"What?"

"Be home by midnight."

The door didn't slam, but almost.

Damn that Dom Paladino. Here he was still causing Sara problems.

4

THE EMERGENCY AT the NoHo renovation turned out to be corroded pipes inside inadequate PVC tape. Evidently the plumber hadn't wanted to go to the trouble of swapping out the pipes themselves, so he'd resorted to cosmetic changes. Dom was more than a little steamed, but Eric, their project manager, had things under control.

Good thing, since Dom had a full day. He needed to stop by the office and have a look at the blueprints for the SoHo apartment complex. Hopefully Luca would be there and they could go over the plans for Tony's bachelor party. Then Dom had an appointment for a trim before his interview at Edelman PR, which he was looking forward to. The great thing about working at such a large firm was that they had offices all over the world. The downside? He'd be a small cog in a huge machine.

Half a block ahead of him, he noticed a dark-haired woman wearing jeans and a tucked-in T-shirt. It took all of a second to be certain it was Sara. He'd memorized that curvy behind.

He noticed the canvas bag she was carrying and had a hunch she was going to the same place he was headed— Met Foods. Walking faster, he made sure he didn't get too close. It would be a shame to let this opportunity pass him by. She still owed him an answer, and while she'd dodged him the other night, he wasn't going to be so quick to let her off the hook this time. Two minutes later he followed her into the store.

After grabbing a bottle of water and a pack of breath mints, he scoped out a couple of aisles before spotting her in the produce section. He planted himself across from her and tried to look engrossed in the nectarines.

"Stalking me now?"

He looked up, pretended to be surprised and said, "Hey."

"What are you doing here?" she asked.

"Um…the same thing you're doing?"

The way she looked at him was like being x-rayed at LaGuardia. She was probably deciding what to say to make a quick escape. Then a glance at his selections made her laugh. "Water and breath mints. I'm actually surprised you don't have cases of mints on hand at all times."

"Meaning?"

"I think you know." Her voice was like rich honey, easy, flowing, made even sweeter by the sly smile that turned up the edges of her lips.

"Dominic?"

The voice came from behind him. Definitely feminine, not completely familiar. Turning, it took him a second to realize it was Danielle Orteaga, a thirtysomething woman he'd met a few times at his gym. She was in great shape, pretty, not afraid to ask for what she wanted. And she was married. Which was enough for Dom to keep her at arm's length. He nodded at her with a noncommittal smile and turned right back to Sara.

"Well, I better get busy so I can make it to the restaurant before the lunch rush," she said.

The drop in temperature only made Dom more determined not to let this serendipitous meeting go to waste. But if he just came out and asked her what he'd done to piss her off, she'd be gone before he could take a second breath. He went around to her side before she could get away and looked in her cart. "So this stuff is all for pizza?"

"And the pasta dishes. Salads. Appetizers. Come on, you know our menu better than I do."

"It threw me when I didn't see any pineapples."

That made her smile change. No trace of sarcasm, which he considered a victory. He wasn't even sure why he was trying so hard. She was hot, of course she was, but if that was all it took, he'd have actually lived up to his reputation.

Sara pushed her cart over to the lettuces, several of which she carefully selected, then on to the radishes. He trailed along, not even trying to make up an excuse, although with everything she had in that cart, he wondered if she'd have to take a taxi back to Moretti's.

Britney Addleson, one of the waitresses from the diner near his apartment, stopped him midstride with a hand on his chest. The move surprised him—it was more forward than he appreciated—but he happened to catch Sara's re-action, and okay, it was worth the intrusion to see that spark of outrage.

"I didn't know you came to this store," Britney said, making sure he was aware of her prominent breasts, snug in her white T-shirt.

"I was just passing by. I have to be at the office in about ten minutes, so I'm going to have to get a move on or be late. See you at the diner."

Britney's shocked expression wasn't satisfying, except that it let him extricate himself without doing too much damage. It wasn't a surprise to see her blush and walk away. The clock, though, had been ticking this whole time, and he couldn't wait much longer to choose his endgame. Confrontation? Or gentle persuasion?

WHY SARA WAS taken aback by the women so blatantly flirting with Dom made zero sense. This was a pattern she'd seen for years, up to and including her own sister.

Just because Sara had hidden her crush successfully didn't mean she was guilt free. Of course, all she'd gotten for her efforts was lethal doses of private and public humiliation. Hard to forget that, even when the conversation seemed so easy between them. Beneath that suave visage, she knew he still had questions, and until she answered him or convinced him the past didn't matter, he'd wear her down. And how she could equate that to sex and be thrilled about it was just plain sick.

For now, though, the smart move was to keep shopping, pretend he wasn't even there. Right behind her. So close that she was feeling slightly giddy. Without a glance his way, she continued going up and down aisles, adding to her cart.

Of course she couldn't help noticing that he looked great. Slim dark dress slacks, a tailored shirt that showed off his physique and what looked like a silk tie. He seemed taller, broader, just since the other night, which told her she'd better get her feet planted and her head out of the clouds.

Sara hadn't realized she'd stopped until he almost rammed into her from behind.

She grabbed the first thing she saw—a can of olives.

"I'm surprised you don't buy that sort of thing in bulk," Dom said.

"Thanks for your concern. I'm shopping for the house, too."

"Ah."

"Why are you still here?"

"Am I making you nervous?" He flashed a smile. "I apologize," he said, taking a step back.

"Make me nervous?" she said with a snort. "I figured you'd go trailing after one of your girlfriends."

"You must have me confused with someone else. No girlfriend."

"Well, whatever you call it," she muttered, and swung around to the next aisle.

He switched to walking beside her. "It?"

Sara sighed loudly and tried not to let his pleasant masculine scent distract her.

"There is one way to get rid of me."

"Yeah? Name it." She bit down on her lip. He'd baited her, and she'd snapped at it. No doubt he was waiting with a smile. She'd be damned if she'd look.

Oh, hell, she should just let him ask his question. Get the whole thing over with.

Somehow her cart headed straight for the checkout. Without any prompting from her. She insisted he go through first. Before she could sigh with relief, he paid for his water and mints and waited at the end of the counter.

Until she started unloading, she hadn't realized she'd overbought by quite so much. She stared at the groceries, trying to think of an elegant way to tell Mr. Stein she wanted to put half of it back. No dice. She was stuck with all of it.

None of it was stupid stuff. Just more than they needed. She'd never be able to walk it all to the restaurant, and she hated spending money on a cab when she should have had two bags, max.

Mr. Stein had already filled her canvas bag and another larger, paper one, and he stared over the top of his thick black-framed glasses at the groceries he had yet to ring up. Bending over slowly, he brought a large box out from under the counter. He scanned the remaining items and packed them into the box.

Sara had her credit card ready when the older man gave her the total.

Mr. Stein lifted a corner of the box, testing the weight. "Sara," he said, "how are you going to carry all of this to the restaurant? You have a cab waiting?"

Dom coughed. Or laughed, it didn't matter.

She slid in her credit card with the utmost lack of concern. "Why should I do that when I've got free labor?" She inclined her head at Dom, without so much as a glance.

Mr. Stein looked over at him. "He's going to ruin his good shirt."

"I'm sure he has more."

No mistaking Dom's laugh this time.

Finally, after she signed the chip machine, she looked at him and smiled. "Although I'll understand if you need to pass. I'm sure it's pretty heavy."

Okay, she deserved the eye roll. When he actually lifted the box, her gaze went straight to his biceps, and she had to swallow real quick, because yes, the guy really did work out. Shit. He'd always had a good body, but now he was even sleeker with broad shoulders and narrow hips.

Aware she was staring, she grabbed the canvas bag. With an amused gleam in his eyes, Mr. Stein glanced from her to Dom, then held out the paper sack for her.

"Lead on, Macduff," Dom said.

Sara opened her mouth, but before she could correct him, he said, "Yeah, I know it's not the original quote, but it was fun watching your nose twitch."

"It did not," she said, shifting the bag in her right arm to a more comfortable position. "Besides, I was going to say I was joking. I can take a cab if you would just help me get the box—"

He laughed and walked out of the store.

She had little choice but to catch up with him.

This whole thing had slipped out of her control. Not in a terrible way, but she most definitely wasn't in her comfort zone. "I thought you had to be somewhere," she said, as they stopped at the corner of Prince Street.

"I do, but not until my one-thirty interview."

"What for?"

"A public relations firm. Oh, and I need to get a trim," he said, straining to get a look at his watch. "Gotta make a good impression."

"I think you're going to do fine in that department," she said, as they reached the end of the block. Any PR firm in the country would be nuts not to hire Dom on the spot.

"Hey, was that a compliment?" Dom said. "Better be careful—you don't want me getting a big head."

"Too late for that."

Dom waited until she met his gaze. "Was that nice?"

His eyes weren't as dark with the morning sunlight bringing out tiny gold flecks. But they were still warm and full of life. She remembered him smiling a lot as a kid. Though why not? He'd had it made even before he'd uttered his first word.

Something else she noticed—he wasn't smiling now.

"I was joking," she muttered and started to cross the street.

A loud honk nearly shattered her eardrums. She'd almost walked right into a passing cab.

She stepped back onto the sidewalk, grateful she hadn't dropped the bags.

"Do me a favor," Dom said.

"What's that?" Reluctantly, she looked at him.

"Get that for me." With a jut of his chin, he glanced up. A lock of dark hair had fallen across his forehead.

Oh, God.

"What do you want me to do with it?"

"Just push it back." He frowned at her as if she was being a twit, which she totally deserved. "Here, give me one of those."

"It's okay. I got it." She shifted the bags until she had a free hand, at least for a few seconds, and swept back the dark silky strands.

She was touching Dominic Paladino's hair. With all the aplomb of a geeky, awkward fifteen-year-old.

The stubborn lock fell forward again.

"Don't be so gentle. Just push it all the way back." He ducked so she could reach the top of his head, and she combed his hair straight back until her fingers were buried completely in the thick mane.

"You should put some stuff in it," she murmured, their faces so close she could feel his warm breath on her cheek. "You know, to keep it in place."

"Like a gel?" He straightened, frowning, and her hand fell away. Just as the bag cradled by her left arm almost did. "Nope. Never gonna happen. I just need a trim."

Foot traffic had picked up in the last few minutes, probably because it was close to lunchtime. And while they weren't blocking the sidewalk, several people sighed dramatically as they skirted them. Others smiled and said hello to Dom.

Sara gasped. *Lunchtime!*

She glanced at Dom's slim gold watch. "Shit."

"What?"

"I need to hurry. The lunch crowd will be coming in soon." She was already on the move, and Dom had no trouble keeping up with her.

When they turned the corner, she spotted the Spicy Meatball food truck parked almost directly in front of Morretti's. Her blood pressure shot through the roof, and before she knew it she was holding on to her bags for dear life and rushing toward the interlopers.

"Hey, Sara. Wait."

She heard Dom, but she didn't have time to stop and explain. He'd see the problem soon enough. Already two people were standing off to the side waiting to order, as the scumbag prepared for the lunch crowd.

"Hey," she said, moving in as close as she could to the truck window. "Again? You have to park right in front of our entrance? That's just taking things too damn far. Come on. Why can't you just go back to where you used to park?"

The guy, who must have been in his midthirties, scruffy and already sweating even though it wasn't that hot out, barely glanced up before he went back to ignoring her.

"I should have you arrested," Sara said. "They'll take your damn license. I bet it's not even legitimate, probably black market."

The man and woman waiting to order moved closer to the window and stared at her, as if they were watching a reality show. Sara didn't care about that, but she wished they'd go away so she didn't have to watch her language. "I'm talking to you," she said, adding, "asshole" at a lower pitch. "What the hell do you think you're doing? There's a whole city for you to sell to. This is how my family makes our living. Don't you have any conscience?"

"I'd like to know that, too," Dom said, suddenly right by her side. His voice was raised, although not quite as loud as hers had gotten.

"Look, I got a right to park here," the guy said. "You do what you gotta do. I do what I gotta do. But if you don't let the customers get to the window, I'm gonna call the cops."

Dom leaned in closer to Sara. "I thought you were going to do that?" He paused to study her, then whispered, "Is he parked legally?"

"What he's doing is wrong, and it's no accident he's parked right here. I've asked him nicely. He ignored me. But this is the third time…"

Dom looked at the guy. "Come on, man. You can clearly see her point. There are other places to park around here. Why do you have to poach on a neighborhood restaurant?"

"Get lost, Popeye. This ain't your business." He turned to the people behind Sara.

"How about *you* get lost?" Sara muttered a curse. "Why do you have to be such a prick?"

Three more people had gotten in line, and Sara was so angry she was ready to stab all of the truck's tires, but that would only keep them in front of the restaurant longer.

"Listen," Dom said, keeping his voice low, and backing her up from the center of the fray. "Why don't you go inside? Put the bags down. Maybe ask Carlo to come get this box. Let me see what I can work out with this schmuck, huh?"

Sara was about to tell him she didn't need to be rescued, but then she saw the second person in the truck. A woman who was staring at Dom as if she'd like to order him for lunch.

"Fine. But if he doesn't budge, I'm going to look up every single possible violation I can call on this guy and I'm going to make him sorry as hell."

"Good idea. Now go. We'll get this straightened out."

With one last vicious glare at the guy and his Dom-struck sidekick, Sara walked inside the restaurant, desperately wanting to drag the growing line of customers behind her. Instead of going to the kitchen, though, she stood at the window. Watching.

A moment later, Jeannette was at her side. "Look at the

coglioni on that guy. He keeps this up, it's gonna put a big dent in the week's revenue."

"My parents are on their first vacation in forever, and he decides to stake a claim outside our door."

Jeannette took one of the bags, then turned around to the counter and shouted for Carlo. One of the other waitresses, Natalie, was taking phone orders.

"What's Dom doing?" Jeannette asked.

"Trying to work something out. Notice the woman who can't take her eyes from him."

"That could work," Jeannette said.

"Maybe."

Carlo rushed past them, out the door, took the box from Dom as if they'd planned the maneuver, then hurried back inside.

Dom didn't even lose a step. For a minute it looked as if the food truck owner was going to do something drastic. In fact, he flicked something at Dom, who stepped aside, shook his head, then kept on talking, looking calm as could be, as if nothing had happened.

Not two minutes later, the owner, the woman, Dom and several customers were all laughing.

Sara exchanged a look with Jeannette, who just shrugged. Then they looked back at the silent show. A few more words, a nod, followed by a handshake.

A goddamn handshake?

Several people at the end of the line peeled away to follow Dom, who held the door open for them. They all seemed pleased to be following their new guru, and surprisingly, she didn't recognize a single person.

Jeannette hustled to get behind the counter, where they really needed Sara, but she couldn't leave yet.

"Okay. We've settled things, and Rocky won't be coming back to this spot again."

"Rocky?"

"I gave him a tip on a better location," Dom said, shrugging.

The relief was instantaneous but riding on its back was a slice of resentment that Mr. Big Shot was able to swoop in and save the day. He just fixed everything with his smile and that ridiculous charisma. Must be swell to be Dominic Paladino.

"Wait," he said. "Did I do something wrong?"

Well, no, how could he?

She closed her eyes, ashamed that she'd let anything other than gratitude show. That she'd lost her temper in front of him. In front of anyone. And that in the end, the biggest shame of her life—the article she'd written—was but a fleeting memory for him. Even though it had haunted her for years.

"No," she said, pulling it together. "You haven't done anything wrong. I'm very grateful this mess won't have to trouble my parents when they get back. Thank you."

"It wasn't a problem," he said, but the tone in his voice had changed. So had the way he was looking at her.

She didn't blame him. Especially when she noticed that his shirt had a big splotch of tomato sauce on the sleeve. The shirt he was supposed to wear to his interview.

"Next five pizzas are on the house," she said, trying to ease the strain.

"I didn't do it for the pizzas," he said, turning to leave.

She caught his arm. That big, muscular arm that tensed even more beneath her hand. "I mean it," she said. "What you did was really kind."

"No sweat," he said, although the easy camaraderie they'd had on their walk had vanished as if it had never existed.

5

FOR THE FIRST time Dom could remember, he'd shown up early for a family dinner. He stood at the living room window of the home he'd grown up in, the same house where his dad had been raised, and where Dom's granddad and great-granddad had been born. The place was a lot bigger now. A room for Nonna, a den with an elaborate sound system, a small backyard where his mom could grow her tomatoes. The patio off the dining room where his father was King of the Grill. And of course their remodeled chef's kitchen—the beating heart of the Paladino family.

Tonight wouldn't be a typical meal. They were going to have an important meeting, which wasn't something that happened often. The last time they'd met in an official capacity had been to discuss Tony taking over the business after their dad's second heart attack. The agenda this evening was to discuss the Paladino Trust. Find a way to make it more relevant to the massive changes Little Italy had undergone since the trust's inception several generations ago.

It had been an inspired idea, one that had been woven into their lives. In a nutshell, the trust was the original rent control, established years before the government had settled on a similar system. But the goal, which had been to help keep the once tight-knit immigrant community close, affordable, safe and thriving, had eroded year by year as the world had evolved. Now, Little Italy was more of an idea than a place: a few blocks, a few stores, a few dozen families who'd descended from the first immigrants was all that remained.

He couldn't see Moretti's three blocks down but that didn't stop his thoughts from going to Sara. Man, had she changed, and not just physically. She'd proven she had a fire inside her back in school when she'd taken the whole faculty to task. Everyone had been stunned by her fierce eloquence, but no one had looked more shocked than Sara herself.

After that day she'd faded into the background again. Although that might have been a reflection of his busy senior year. She'd sure gotten his attention two months later when she'd implied he was the most egregious example of why high school athletics was a complete waste of time and money. That op-ed piece, filled with inflammatory rhetoric, had pissed off a lot more people than him.

Three weeks after that he'd graduated and hadn't thought about her at all. Before going off to college he'd eaten at Moretti's a few times. But Sara had been nowhere in sight.

He pictured her at the order window of the Spicy Meatball, struggling to keep her temper to a controlled roar. Knowing what she could have done without the need for discretion, he respected her effort.

What he didn't understand was her reaction to his assistance. He hadn't been trying to dis her in any way; surely she must have known that. He'd just wanted to ease the situation, turn the argument into a win. There was no reason for her to have been so prickly about it.

Right in the middle of his interview, he'd thought about the resentful way she'd looked at him when he told her about the solution. He'd snapped out of it quickly, but damn. He couldn't afford to have that kind of distraction.

He'd left Edelman with the promise of a follow-up interview, but he didn't have enough of a feel for the big PR firm to know if he'd move forward.

Regardless, he couldn't spend time wondering about Sara. All this attitude was most likely connected to the mysterious *thing* that had happened when they were kids. After racking his brain he couldn't come up with anything. Other than she might've made it up because he'd called her on the article.

Dom saw a cab stop in front and Tony got out. His brother was probably looking forward to tonight. For once, they weren't going to discuss wedding preparations, the guest list, anything to do with nuptials. Compared to that, a multimillion dollar trust was a walk in the park.

It would be like old times. Just the immediate family, no Catherine, no April. Even Nonna was having dinner next door with her friend. Which was good, because it would be a lot easier to talk without having to explain the convoluted evolution of the trust. Hell, it would've taken all night. And the women all understood they weren't being slighted.

"What the hell?" Luca said, poking his head into the living room. "Dom's here on time? Call the *Times*."

"On time?" his mom called out from the kitchen. "He was here early."

Tony stopped in the foyer. "What happened? You sick? In trouble? Did you get a girl in trouble?"

Dom wanted to line up his brothers and slap them both silly. "Shut up," he said, and went to the kitchen. "Ma, I'm gonna pour some Chianti. You want some?"

She patted his cheek and smiled at him as if he was

still ten, even though she had to look up to meet his eyes. "Get me and your father some iced tea. And you boys don't drink too much until after we talk." She looked at Tony, then Luca, then at the doorway that led to the dining room.

Luca moved first. "I've got the silver."

Tony didn't say a word, just went to get plates and salad bowls. Dom headed for the wet bar and poured some wine for the three of them.

"Ten bucks says chicken parmesan," Luca said, doling out settings.

"You're on." Dom nodded, keeping his expression neutral. Luca didn't need to know he'd already asked. "I bet you it's chicken, but she's doing something else with it. Something light for Pop."

"I can smell the sauce."

Dom grinned. "Double or nothing?"

Luca frowned as he picked up the copy of the trust by his place setting. "You did this?"

"Yeah, so?" Knowing his parents, it was inevitable they'd find something to argue about, so Dom had made copies so everyone would have their own set in their hot little hands.

Luca looked at Tony. "Our little brother's growing up."

Dom smacked him on his way back to the kitchen to get the iced tea.

Dinner was on the table ten minutes later, and Luca slipped the ten spot over along with a serving of salad.

"So why don't we all read the first two pages while we have the antipasto?" Dom suggested. "Then we can talk."

His father, Joe, who'd finally taken his seat, looked at Dom. "You got a date after?"

He just smiled, though it had occurred to Dom that if the meeting ended around nine he might bump into Sara on her way home. She'd be walking in this direction so it wouldn't seem weird. But for all he knew, she wasn't even working.

Although, why would he bother when he was still pissed at her?

Dom read the pages of the antiquated agreement, as if he didn't already know most of it by heart. The last time it had been amended was back in the 1950s, and that was something their attorney—Great-uncle Peter—had suggested to protect the family in case of a lawsuit.

The room was quiet as they all read, except for the occasional sound of crunched vegetables. The language took some concentration, having originated in the early twentieth century, but the basics were straightforward.

"Okay." Theresa put down her paper. "Let's finish eating first," she said. "Talk after. Give us time to digest. The last thing your father needs is *agita*."

"I'm fine, Theresa. Enough. If the boys want to talk about the trust, let them."

"I don't know how everything has gotten so complicated," she said. "Attorneys and accountants, and the way you boys have had to keep things so private." Her gaze went to Tony and Luca. "It almost cost you Catherine and April. I don't want that happening to Dominic, or your future children."

"That's why we're meeting, Ma," Luca said. "We all agree. Look at this stuff." He waved the document so close to his wineglass he nearly knocked it over. "This was written for a different world. I'm not saying we should change the current rents, but I think it's time we stop buying properties."

"Can't argue with that," Tony said. "We don't have to kick anyone out. Just stop adding to the problem."

"So, we'd stop altogether?" Dom asked.

"Not necessarily," Tony said. "We could set parameters.

For instance, if half the co-ops in a building are already owned by outsiders, we walk away."

"I'm not saying we shouldn't stop." Dom picked up his wine. "Not at all."

They all got quiet for a while, chewing on more than the food.

"You were right, Dominic," Joe said, looking at him and nodding slowly, as he always did when trying to access his memory. "What was it, two years ago? When you told me we were missing the bigger picture."

Everyone stared at Dom.

"Tell them," Joe said, gesturing expansively. "Tell them how you think we could do better with the money. I should have listened then."

Dom set his wineglass down. "First of all, I doubt anyone could have foreseen how much the trust would grow. We have a lot of money sitting around." Tony opened his mouth, and Dom said, "Yes, I know it's all invested. And making even more money than we'd ever spend in five lifetimes. Let me rephrase—there are plenty of uses for the funds all around us. The community isn't what it used to be but we can improve what's left of it."

"Don't be too generous," Theresa said. "Most of it belongs to you boys. I know you won't spend it, but make sure you leave enough for my grandchildren."

Dom and Luca both smiled.

Tony laughed. "Not a problem, Ma. So don't you worry."

"I was at Collect Pond Park this morning," Joe said, "and I'll tell you right now, it's not what it could be, even though they finally figured out how to get the pond back. On such a beautiful spring day, it should have been filled with people, but it's mostly concrete, and it needs more green. More trees. More places to sit, tables to play chess, more children and dogs. It's ugly, surrounded by government buildings. Nobody wants to go there."

Tony put down his fork. "We can change the terms of the trust however we want," he said, and glanced at Dom. "I think you and Pop are on to something. We should honor the community that used to be here. When Little Italy meant something. Fix the park. Show people what it used to mean."

"It was called Five Points at one time," Theresa said. "Used to be the worst slum in America."

"And then it got better." Joe took another bite of chicken and turned to Theresa. "This isn't too bad, even though it could use some marinara and mozzarella."

"Don't forget the parmesan, and it should also be fried."

Theresa gave Luca a look that shut him right up. "Excuse me for wanting my husband here more than I want parmesan."

"That's love, my boys," Joe said. "Remember that."

"Anyway," Theresa said, her brow creasing. "What I want to know is what we're going to tell people. It could be a real mess if they find out what the Paladinos have—"

"Who says we have to say anything?" Dom thought for a minute as he poured himself a little more wine. "We let the attorney continue to take care of the properties and the rents through the management company, and just funnel funds into something new. Something we don't have to hide if we don't want to."

Tony nodded. "Like a public works fund."

"Tell them the rest, Dom," Joe said. "About the matching funds. It's a good idea."

Dom was more than a little surprised his dad had remembered. He hadn't been all that interested when Dom had first broached the subject. "It's not a big deal. But if we're looking to improve public property, we have to get government approval so we should find out if they'd be willing to match whatever we put in."

"Huh." Luca grinned. "Here I thought you were just another pretty face."

Dom slyly flipped him off with a move he'd perfected at sixteen. Luca laughed. He'd only been joking, but somehow it didn't sit well with Dom. Why was he being so damn touchy?

"DeSalvio Playground," Joe said. "That's another place there should be more grass. And the neighborhood could use a good day care center that doesn't cost an arm and a leg."

Theresa frowned at him. "How did you get to be such an expert?"

"I listen when I go to the park," he said. "When I go to the corner for coffee. I hear what's going on."

"You mean, you flirt with all the women?"

"Well," Tony said, "I think the whole idea of focusing on the community in general is a good idea. Why don't we see what we can do? Talk to the accountant. Although Dom's right, we've got a lot of money at our disposal. Dom, you're gonna need to figure out what you want for your own place eventually, but after that? We all have what we need. The company is going fine. Let's figure out where we can make the most difference."

"I can do that," Joe said. "Figure those things out."

No one said anything for a few seconds.

"What? It's not like work. There's no stress in finding out. I like finding out."

Theresa glanced over at Dom. "Maybe you could do that with your father?"

Tony cleared his throat. "Uh, Dom's going on interviews now, so maybe he doesn't have time—"

"Dom is sitting right here," Dom said. "And Pop, if you'd let me, I'd like to work on this with you."

Joe smiled in a way Dom hadn't seen in ages. This new focus of the trust money could be a great project for him. It would keep him involved without harming his health.

"I'd like that, Dominic."

The whole family lifted their glasses, wine and tea. Dom had thought tonight would be complicated and full of arguments. But it seemed they were all ready to finally enter the twenty-first century.

A quick glance at his watch, and Dom knew if he stuck around to clear the table and made plans to meet with his dad in a couple of days, he'd be just in time to catch Sara after she locked up at the pizzeria. Assuming she was working.

Tonight, he wasn't going to let things get away from him. Once and for all, he was going to find out what he'd done that had been so bad she'd carried it around for all these years.

After they'd had dessert, Dom collected the dirty plates, feeling a little nostalgic as he carried them into the kitchen. Now that he was living in Tony's apartment, he didn't see the family as often. Soon enough he'd have a whole different kind of life, separate from Paladino & Sons Construction, the family dinners, the rhythm of generations that had cocooned the brothers since birth.

He thought he might like to stay in New York, but if he ended up with a big PR firm, he'd have to go where they sent him. Maybe some new scenery wouldn't be so bad.

"Hey." Luca had followed close behind, balancing the serving platters and salad bowl. "You knew all along we were having that chicken dish."

Dom grinned. He set the dishes on the counter by the

sink and reached in his pocket. "Here," he said, holding out the ten. "I was gonna give it back to you."

"Yeah, sure." Luca set down his load and snatched the bill. "Shithead."

They looked at each other and laughed. Roughly speaking, they were worth close to a hundred million dollars each. Ten bucks would hardly break either one of them.

6

THE NIGHT WAS balmy and it felt good to move after eating two servings of his mom's raspberry panna cotta. Dom tried to decide if he should take the subway or cab it home. On a pleasant night like this? Had to be the subway. Even if he did have to walk past Moretti's.

It was just after nine, but he didn't care if the restaurant was closed or not, or even if Sara had worked tonight. Sometime between dessert and leaving the house he'd decided he didn't want to get sucked into any more of her bullshit.

If she didn't want to tell him what he'd done to her, fine. She could keep her little secret. He wasn't about to screw up another interview worrying about her, or miss the chance to enjoy working with his dad. Dom looked forward to spending one-on-one time with him.

And using the trust to give Little Italy a cosmetic boost sounded right. No telling what might come of it. Maybe more of Dom's generation would stick around. Just because he'd probably be heading down a different road himself didn't mean that he'd stop caring about the old neighborhood.

A blond couple he didn't recognize was strolling toward him. As they got closer he gave them a friendly nod, which they ignored, then entered the five-story building that now consisted of luxury apartments. Before the conversion, Dom had known every family who'd lived there.

A block away from Moretti's he spotted Sara locking the door, the light inside revealing the stacked chairs on top of the tables. Oh, well, he wouldn't be rude. He'd say hi as he passed her. She could acknowledge him or not; he didn't care.

Between Dom and the restaurant, two guys crossed the street, darting directly in front of a car like idiots. One of them looked like Kenny Tomlinson, which made sense because being a dick was right up Tomlinson's alley.

Dom watched the two guys loop around so they were behind Sara, who hadn't noticed them. He didn't like the looks of that.

Kenny didn't even know Sara, so why was he…?

Alarm bells went off, and Dom's gut tightened. That wasn't Kenny. Dom started jogging, making sure when he crossed the street that he didn't call attention to himself.

As he got closer, Dom realized he had no idea who those dudes were. They didn't look like tourists. What they did look like was trouble.

When the tall guy with the bleached hair got up next to Sara, she jolted, reared back.

Screw jogging, Dom flat out ran until he pushed himself between the stranger and Sara and put an arm around her shoulders. "Sorry I'm late, sweetheart," he said, feeling the waves of tension roll through her body. "Who's your friend?"

The guy stepped back, and Sara relaxed a little. "Hi," she murmured with a shaky smile.

"Hi back," Dom said, then kissed her right on the mouth. She tensed all over again, and so did he. While he'd just been trying to make a point, the kiss had caught him by surprise. It wasn't just lips on lips, which should have been nothing. Instead, it was a *kiss*. Even though there was no tongue involved, he felt as if he'd closed a circuit, letting a spark flow between them. It lasted seconds, but the effects lingered after he pulled back.

Then one of the idiots ruined everything by bumping into Dom's back.

"What are you doing with pretty boy, gorgeous?" Blondie said. "Me and my buddy, we got what you want." He used his elbow this time to try and move Dom out of the way.

At the same time, the other scumbag had sidled up to Sara's right, but instead of looking at her, his focus was on her bag. Did they think she kept the restaurant's cash in that purse? The strap was across her body, but Dom knew from the guy's body language that he must have a knife at the ready. A practiced snatch and grab.

Pulling Sara in closer, Dom stared straight into the guy's blemished face. "You're not from around here. I suggest you go back to wherever you came from."

Both men laughed.

Not men. Boys. Barely out of high school, Dom guessed. After repeating every grade twice. Definitely not from around here. Blondie's bleached hair was spiked. Both earlobes were plugged, and an ugly sleeve of tattoos ran down his left arm. The other guy, whom Dom had mistaken for Kenny, wasn't so flashy. But he had a hell of a mean look in his eyes, which hadn't drifted far from his target.

Beside Dom, Sara squirmed free of his arm. "What is this, Dom?" Her tone was incredulous, her accusing gaze searching him instead of watching out for the two thugs who were seconds away from robbing her. "Did you set this up? Just because I didn't let you walk me home last we—"

A fist slammed into his face. He staggered back, but

wasted no time in landing a jab to Blondie's nose. Dom grabbed Sara's arm, lurching her forward. By the time she was out of range, he was already halfway into his round kick, which caught the other guy right over the liver.

He grunted in pain and stumbled back against the brick building.

"Oh, shit!"

That was Sara's voice, loud, surely gaining more attention from anyone nearby, but Dom wasn't going to let up until cops stepped in or these idiots made a run for it. His next jab hit Blondie's nose in the same place. Blood gushed out, sliding down his chin and onto his shirt as he cursed violently.

Dom thought he saw the flash of a knife in the other guy's hand, still ready to slash the purse strap, or worse. "Get out of here, Sara. Now."

A quick flat kick to the groin, and the resulting scream almost covered the sound of a small switchblade hitting the sidewalk. By that time, Blondie, trying to staunch the blood streaming down his face, was already making a run for it. His buddy followed, holding his crotch, groaning in pain and throwing one last death glare at Dom.

SARA, STILL REELING after the quickest fight in Little Italy history, gasped when Dom turned around. His eye was already swelling, and blood trickled down from the edge of his eyebrow. It seemed stupidly obvious now that he hadn't set anything up, and she felt like an idiot for even thinking—

"You okay?" he asked.

"Me? I'm fine. He had a knife. I didn't know he had a knife."

Dom grunted as he picked up the weapon, pressing it closed against his belt. "I realize."

"Oh, God, Dom… I'm so sorry. I feel terrible. Thank you for—"

"Didn't do it for you." He stared after the two creeps. "Pretty boy," he muttered under his breath. "Stupid fuckers."

Sara almost laughed. If those two ever came sniffing around again, well, she just hoped Dom wasn't the one who got arrested. "Come on. We've got a first aid kit at the restaurant."

"I'll be fine. Let's get you home."

"You're bleeding. And the parlor is right there."

He touched a finger to the cut, and looked at the red spot, which was tiny. "I'm going to walk you home anyway, so let's go now so I can get back to my place while ice will still make a difference."

She was making things worse with every word. God, why was it so complicated with him? "Right. You're right." She took hold of the back of his arm and started moving toward home as quickly as she could. Would it be smarter to stop a cab? Even as she doubted it, she maneuvered him closer to the curb.

"We don't need a taxi. I've been hurt lots worse, trust me."

"You fight? I mean, you fight willingly?"

"I skirmish. I train. That's not fighting."

"Is that how…" Everything had happened in a matter of seconds. "How did you learn all those moves?"

He gave her half a grin. "Years of classes."

She nodded as they crossed the street. They'd reach her house in a few minutes. Her folks were still in Italy, and Ellie wouldn't be home until eleven, so Sara could take care of Dom's face without having to confess her role in getting him beat up. "Luckily, I put a big rib eye in the fridge this morning."

"What? Why is that lucky?"

"Because of your…" She almost caught him in the ribs. If he hadn't ducked, she would have gotten him. Obviously he was tender there, as well.

"You know that's not really…a steak isn't necessary. Ice is good. Personally, I prefer a bag of frozen peas."

"I know. I was just… I don't know what I was thinking." Sara sighed. "Wait. Personal preference? How often do you get beat up?"

He stopped and stared at her. "Beat up? I took a punch. That's it."

"Sorry," she said, and tugged him along. "What happened to your ribs? Did one of those guys—"

Shaking his head, he glanced down. "I think I pulled a muscle when I pushed you out of the way." His gaze lifted to her face, then slid down to her arm. "I grabbed you pretty hard. Did I hurt you?"

"No." She swallowed at the concern in his face before looking away. "No, you didn't. You saved me from being robbed. And maybe worse. Thank you," she whispered.

"I'm sorry you had to go through that."

She looked at him, briefly, glad his cut didn't look too bad, and then stared straight ahead. All he seemed to do was confuse her. For so long, she'd thought he was an arrogant jerk who never had to lift a finger to get what he wanted.

At last, they'd reached her parents' duplex. They took the three steps up to the porch, and just as he'd done a few other times along the way, Dom glanced around behind them.

Sara laughed a little and got a frown. "Dom, they think you're my boyfriend," she said. "I promise they won't be back."

He gave her a slow, sexy smile. "I don't know. They were pretty stupid."

"That's true." She met his eyes and steeled herself against a tingling sensation that started in her belly and was spreading through her thighs. No, he hadn't given *her* a sexy smile. That was just the way he smiled. Damn him.

"Go ahead," he said, nodding at the door. "I'll wait until you're inside and locked up."

"What do you mean? You're coming inside with me."

He shook his head. "I'm going to take a cab home. I live fifteen minutes away."

"And you'll still live the same fifteen minutes away after I tend to your eye."

Images of how he'd gone all superhero on those stupid bastards looped in slow motion in her mind, and by the time she'd gotten her key out, her heart was racing like a Lamborghini.

Jesus, what did the poor guy have to do to prove he wasn't that shitty kid she'd overheard talking to his friends a lifetime ago? He let her get away with a slapdash apology after she'd been really bitchy. Got rid of the food truck and hadn't even been pissed that he'd had to change clothes before his interview—while she'd acted like an ungrateful jerk. Then he saved her from who knows what kind of assault with Bruce Lee moves and James Bond finesse. Right after her cynicism had gotten him punched in the first place.

The pattern was… Well, yeah.

She unlocked the front door and led him straight into the kitchen. To have the place to herself was rare, and she didn't even give a damn that tonight had been slated as a prime transcribing opportunity. "I'll get the peas and then we'll go to the bathroom so I can put something on that cut."

After grabbing the frozen vegetables, she led him through the living room and up the stairs. Across from her bedroom was the bathroom. It was comfortably large, and while she pulled out the first aid kit from inside the vanity, he sat down on the bathtub surround.

She put the antiseptic and a small Band-Aid on the countertop, and then washed her hands as the water heated up for the washcloth. "Close your eyes," she said, her voice low, her concentration high. It really was a minor cut, but she got it completely clean and medicated before she covered the wound.

Dom didn't even wince.

She went to put the peas on his eye.

"Thanks. I can take it from here," he said.

"Of course you can." She took two steps back before turning to the sink. She honestly felt clumsier than anytime since she'd gotten her braces. "I should have a look at your ribs."

"Nah, they're okay—" He stopped, and after a brief silence he said, "Yeah, maybe you should."

Sara bit her lip. His voice had lowered and now she wasn't sure she could turn around and face him.

"You'll have to help me get my shirt off. I want to keep icing this eye."

"Or I could just lift it and have a look."

"You could."

She was the one who'd opened her big mouth. No way was she going to back down and let him know how much he affected her. Washing her hands a second time, she said, "Well, you were right about the neighborhood. It makes me sad, though. Growing up, it always felt as if we were in a separate village outside of the Big Apple. You know?"

"Yeah. Everything's changed now. The real estate market, the massive push to modernize. Everyone wants to cash in."

"Must be good for business." She turned around in time to see him nod.

"We're busy, all right," he said, and yanked his shirt from his jeans.

Her heart nearly catapulted out of her chest. "Before we—" She cleared her throat. "Again, thank you," she said, hoping he couldn't detect the slight tremor in her voice. "I have no idea what I would have done if you hadn't been there."

Taking her hand, he tugged her down to sit beside him. "You already thanked me. No more, okay?" He smiled and tucked a lock of hair behind her ear. "Maybe you can help me unbutton my shirt. It's kind of fitted so just pulling it up will be tough."

The shirt looked tailor-made, and the buttons were on the small side. Unfastening them would be difficult with her unsteady fingers, but she was game.

Inhaling his rich earthy scent, Sara wetted her lips and freed the first button.

What were they doing here? He hadn't actually hurt his ribs. They both knew it.

She unfastened the second button and thought of Robert. As confusing as their relationship often was, she could at least make some sense of it. They'd both been journalism students, he'd had an obsession with the Vatican and Sara spoke Italian a lot better than he did. Their plan was that she'd join him in Rome as soon as she finished her thesis. But by then Robert would be established and probably wouldn't need her at all.

God, what was wrong with her? When had she become this cynical?

They had a lot more in common. They'd even had some fun times…

"My ribs are fine," Dom said, covering her hand with his free one. "You don't have to do this."

"What?" Sara met his eyes. "Did I— I don't understand."

A resigned smile curved his mouth. "You're thinking awfully hard. And I bet they aren't pleasant thoughts." He let go of her hand and started to rise.

She gripped his arm and held firm. "Please don't," she said. "I wasn't very gracious the other day when you took care of the food truck. I don't have a good excuse. I don't even know why I acted that way, but it's really bothered me." She paused to take a breath, not sure how much longer she could maintain eye contact with him. "I'm so grateful my dad won't have to stress out over that damn truck, I can't even tell you. Moretti's is all they really have, and it makes me crazy to think they could lose it."

"I was glad to help," he said, and stroked her cheek with his thumb. "So let's forget about it, okay?"

"No, it's not okay. I don't— I can't just—"

Wariness flickered as his eyes narrowed. He lowered his hand. "I'm not looking for anything in return. You understand that, don't you?"

"What?" She blinked. Had a horrible thought. "No. God. Of course not." A laugh escaped her. "As if any woman would…" She trailed off, unsettled by the flash of annoyance in his eyes. "Are you saying that because I'm jittery?" She gave him no time to respond. "Look, the kiss was fake. I know that, okay? But I—I liked it. And I just said that out loud so I might have to kill myself." Sara sighed and slumped back against the wall. "The truck would've been so much easier for my parents to deal with than a funeral."

Dom was clearly trying to hold back a laugh. "You have anything decent to drink?"

She nodded. "I do, in fact. Something very good." She stood and headed for the door. "Why don't you come with me?"

He followed the short distance to her bedroom. She motioned to her thankfully made bed while she unboxed a bottle of Jameson Gold Reserve Irish Whiskey she'd received as a moving-away gift. "Neat? On the rocks?"

"I'm good," he said. "Pour yourself a shot. Or two."

"That bad, huh?"

He just smiled, and she stared down at her trembling hand.

"Part of this has to do with what happened with those guys," she said, avoiding his eyes.

"I'm sure that's most of it."

Damn him. Why couldn't he be the jerk she'd always imagined? Yeah, two shots sounded like a very good idea. She needed to calm down. And to keep her mouth shut. As if almost being mugged wasn't bad enough, Dominic was in her bedroom. On her bed. Looking sexy as hell with his shirt yanked from his jeans, while she still couldn't quite get over the fact that he'd helped ruin her senior year, which almost cost her a place at GWU.

And now here she was blaming the victim. When she knew damn well her editorial had been the root cause of all her grief.

"It's a great whiskey. I don't bring it out except for special occasions."

"Like watching me get clocked?"

Mentally wincing, she grabbed her water glass from the nightstand and opened the bottle. "Tell me about those kung fu classes you took," she said, pouring in two fingers, then letting the aroma of molasses and almonds linger before she took a sip.

He smiled and took the bag away from his eye. "When I was a little kid I got bullied a lot."

"You?"

He nodded. "I was always getting fawned over by teachers and parents. Everyone kept saying I should be on TV or something because I was cute as a bug. Which, in case anyone ever asks, isn't a compliment to a seven-year-old. It also didn't help that I had a lisp. It got pretty bad."

"That's awful."

"My mom got me a speech therapist. Eventually the lisp cleared up, which was actually more about my teeth than a real impediment. But my father enrolled me in a karate class, which helped even more."

She tried not to stare at his chest exposed by the two undone buttons. "Did you do a lot of fighting back then?"

"Nah. Because I knew I could win, and my classmates discovered that real quick. Although I didn't stop at karate. I didn't compete in school, but I got into mixed martial arts. I still go to the dojo, although I'm not that into it anymore. It's a tough sport, and I don't like getting hurt."

"Yeah, well, it'll help if you keep your distance from me. I seem to be a trouble magnet when it comes to you."

He stared at her, his lips slightly parted, his gaze probing. She hid behind her drink, but that didn't faze him.

"What did I do to you?" he asked. "I've been trying to figure it out, but I can't. I don't like not knowing."

Any relaxation the whiskey had afforded her vanished, replaced by a panic that jumbled her thoughts and made her want to run from the room. Instead, she leaned across the short distance between them and kissed him right on the lips.

7

Dom INHALED AS her lips moved against his. His response might have been delayed, but not unenthusiastic. He'd wanted to kiss Sara since he'd first seen her at Moretti's, but with her hot-and-cold attitude toward him, he'd been pretty convinced it was a lost cause.

He reached for her hand and pulled her down to sit beside him. He swept a hand down her back all the way to her waist as he got a feel for what she liked. A soft sexy sound inspired him to explore her mouth slowly, thoroughly, and she seemed to enjoy a tease here and there.

It didn't take long to let go of his thoughts and concentrate on her taste, now that the whiskey was gone. Enjoy the feel of her slender back under his hand, and the scent of something delicate and flowery when he nuzzled her just behind her ear.

Her hand moved up on his thigh. He reacted with a jerk, but not in a place she would have felt. Accepting her boldness as an invitation, he cupped a hand over her breast.

"Oh," she whispered, the warmth of her breath gentle across his cheek.

"Okay?" he asked, slipping his fingers underneath her

T-shirt. The first contact with her smoo... his pulse into a frenzy.

"This is crazy," she whispered, one second be... kissed him again, harder, her tongue pushing its way pa... his lips into his mouth.

Heat shot through him. Groaning, he cupped her bra-covered breast, the nipple poking his palm stirring all kinds of sensations inside him. Deepening the kiss, he swirled his tongue around hers, then teased her lower lip with his teeth.

Carefully, giving her plenty of time to stop him, he traced the edge of her bra to the front clasp, which he unhooked in a miraculously smooth move. Then he had her lush flesh filling his hand, the silky skin making him moan with want.

Instead of chasing him away, her fingers found his remaining shirt buttons, and as they switched positions so he could kiss her in every possible way, she moved down button by button until she'd reached his belt.

Her next move made his cock press against his fly. Her delicate hand brushed his chest, ran lightly over his nipples, up his neck, then down again, circling, teasing. Goddammit, he wanted them naked, now.

He grasped her wrist and pulled her arm up so he could slip off her T-shirt. For a moment, he just stared at her pink cheeks, her moist lips, then down to the stunning breasts that he wanted to know much better.

"Now you," she said, easily twisting her hand free so she could push his shirt off his shoulders.

He let her finish taking off his shirt but then caught her hand when she went for his belt. "Wait," he said, looking into her sparkling eyes. "Let me look at you."

Sara tensed a little, hunched her shoulders slightly forward and let out a nervous laugh. He wanted to say something to reassure her. Tell her how beautiful she was, but somehow he didn't think it was the right thing to say. Both of her rosy pink nipples stood out and nothing short of an earthquake could've stopped him from touching them.

He thumbed the right one, and she shivered.

"I forgot to check your ribs," she whispered, and he laughed.

A blush spread across her face, her lashes sweeping the top of her cheeks, and he had the oddest flash of memory, of that shy teenage girl she'd been ten years ago. Sara looked and sounded different but she still had that bashful streak in her.

Not without regret, he moved his hand from her breast and lifted her chin. "You must've had a tough time in college," he said, drawing a finger across her lush bottom lip.

With a slight frown, she met his eyes. "Not really."

"Don't tell me you weren't chasing men off left and right." He smiled when she laughed. "No use lying to me, I won't believe it."

"Now I'm really worried about your head. You must have a concussion," she said, leaning forward for a kiss.

"Nothing wrong with my head, Sara." He brushed his lips over hers, his mouth and body craving more. "Or my eyesight." He couldn't stand another second without tasting her, and then he was going to kiss her, and keep kissing and touching her until she understood exactly what she was doing to him.

His impatient cock was damn hard, but it would have to wait—well, as long as his brain was still functioning. He swept his tongue inside the moist recesses of her mouth, probing, teasing and inviting her to play.

Until he thought he heard a sound.

Sara didn't react so he was probably wrong.

There it was again, and this time Sara stiffened.

They broke apart.

"I think that was the kitchen door," she whispered, then fell silent while they listened.

A voice floated up the stairs and into the bedroom. "Sara?"

She froze. "Shit. Ellie." Sara sprang to her feet, pulling her bra together with clumsy fingers.

He rose, tried to help her, but she slapped him away. As he was debating whether he could get it together enough to shut the door quietly or if he should just grab his shirt and run for the bathroom, he heard the stairs creak.

"Hurry up," Sara whispered in what was tantamount to a verbal slap across the face.

He hurried. Buttoning as fast as he could, willing his erection to deflate like a pricked balloon, although his body had other ideas.

She had her shirt on, and presumably her bra but everything had happened in a flash, and now she was doing something to her hair.

Dom quickly turned around. Looking at Sara wasn't helping tame his arousal. Then Sara grabbed him by the front of his shirt and dragged him out of the bedroom into the bathroom.

One second later, Ellie was in the hallway. "Sara?"

"I'm here," she said, exhaling as she pasted a smile on her face. "Just getting Dom straightened away."

"Dom?"

Ellie sounded as if she was right outside the bathroom door. There was no hope of doing anything more. If he ignored his condition, then hopefully everyone else would, too.

"Yeah," Sara said. "I can still hardly believe it, but I was almost attacked coming home from work. Dom stepped in and got hammered for his trouble."

"What?"

Dom followed Sara to the hallway. "I wouldn't say hammered. More like a lucky punch." He'd left the damn peas in her bedroom. "It's nothing serious," he said, lightly probing the area around his eye for good measure.

"We've got to talk, though," Sara said, blinking at Ellie. "No more walking home alone. Not for any of us. These guys weren't from the neighborhood. One of them had a knife."

"A small knife." Dom watched Ellie's wide-eyed gaze skitter back and forth between him and Sara. "Like I told Sara, I'm pretty sure their plan was to cut her purse strap and make a run for it."

"Luckily, I didn't have much cash on me, but still…" Sara turned to Dom. "I think you'll be okay," she said, "but you should probably ice that eye when you get home."

He nodded. "Good idea." Over her shoulder, he saw that Ellie's mouth was still open, her eyes wide, and now she was staring so hard at Dom he felt sure she'd seen the bulge behind his fly.

"Let me just rinse my hands," he said. "Then I'll take off."

"Okay," Sara said, too quickly.

He hid in the bathroom, willing away the last of his erection. Dammit, he wished Sara would take a hint and walk Ellie downstairs.

"What the hell?" Ellie said.

"I'll explain more after he leaves," Sara said, barely keeping her voice to a whisper. "Just give me a minute to walk him out."

"Yeah, right. You do that."

Dom left the bathroom, then he and Sara walked in the most innocent way possible to the end of the hall and down the stairs. Neither of them said a word until they got to the front door. Sara put her hand on the knob but he stopped her from turning it.

"Wait a minute," he said. "We have unfinished business."

Her eyes widened and her hand went to her throat. "Are you crazy?" she whispered.

"Not that. You were going to tell me what I did—"

"Oh, God, Dom. Not now."

"Now. I won't let you brush me off." He waited while she glanced at the stairs, assuring herself Ellie wasn't there. "I'm not leaving until you tell me."

She gaped at him as if he'd slapped her, but that was okay because he was just now realizing all that kissing was probably her way of weaseling out of answering him.

"The spring dance," she said, barely opening her jaw enough to get the words out.

"Spring dance?" he repeated, his brain struggling for context. "When?"

"I was thirteen. You were a freshman in high school."

Nothing clicked. "Hell, that was a long time ago."

"I know. I told you to forget about it—it's stupid." She started to pull the door open.

Dom pushed it closed. "It's not stupid. I can tell you're upset."

"I'm upset because of…" She lowered her voice to a whisper. "Ellie."

"I get that. Let's stick to the spring dance."

Sara's anguished sigh almost made him back off. But it also made him more anxious to understand what had happened. Left to fill in the blanks on his own would kill him. So he waited, hating the grim look on her face. He was a second away from giving in and leaving when she finally spoke.

"It was the dance our mothers wanted us to go to. Together."

"Okay." He was still drawing a blank. If he remembered correctly, matchmaking had been a favorite pastime of every mother in the neighborhood. "What about it?"

"You didn't want to take me. Which was understandable. But not when I was thirteen. I was still the obedient daughter who did whatever my parents told me."

"So you were disappointed we didn't end up going together?" He still wasn't clear how that made him the bad guy. He hadn't asked her to go, and then reneged.

Shaking her head, Sara wrung her hands together. "It's what I overheard you say to your friends..."

That landed in his gut. He'd hate to think he was too big of an asshole when he was fourteen, but it was hard to know for sure.

"Fair warning," Ellie said. "I'm coming downstairs now."

They both heard the steps creak.

Dom met Sara's eyes. "We're not done with this," he said. "I need to hear it all. But I am sorry."

She nodded, swung the door open and practically shoved him out.

Jesus, he knew it wouldn't be easy to hear, but he had to know. Especially if it was something that would always keep Sara just out of his reach.

AFTER SARA LOCKED the door and turned around, she found Ellie standing on the second step, arms folded and glaring.

"Did you get a prom dress?" she asked, her mind still on Dom and the puzzled look on his face as he left. "Isn't that why you went shopping?"

"Did you know Dom was coming over tonight?" Ellie countered. "Is that why you gave me a later curfew?"

"Don't be silly." Sara shook her head and went to the kitchen. She was so not in the mood for this crap. Of course she didn't want Ellie thinking something had happened between her and Dom, but Sara had offered a perfectly acceptable explanation. No reason her sister shouldn't accept it.

God, he must think she was such a twit, reacting over something that happened half a lifetime ago. She poured herself some water when she should've gone straight to her bedroom and taken another gulp of whiskey.

Ellie had followed her and leaned a hip against the counter, watching her guzzle half the glass. Her defiant expression was pissing Sara off.

She thought about reminding Ellie she was only seventeen and what Sara did or didn't do was none of her business. But Ellie had that crush on Dom and there was no point in getting into a no-win argument with her.

Sara took a deep breath and checked her tone of voice. "So, no dress?"

Ellie shook her head. "I didn't see one I liked."

"Where are you going to look next?"

"I don't know."

"When's the prom?"

"Four weeks."

"You still have time," Sara said, and feeling more relaxed, gave her sister a smile, which Ellie didn't return.

She wasn't glaring, though, just staring. "You really were attacked?"

"Almost. Like I said, Dom stepped in."

"How could he just *step in*? He must've been with you."

Sara shook her head. "He was coming from his parents' house to the subway. The two guys were walking behind me. He saw them getting too close. I feel terrible he got hurt. But I was lucky he acted quickly."

Ellie still didn't look convinced, but that was just tough. What Sara had told her was the truth. How Dom ended up in the upstairs bathroom was perfectly logical. Hearing herself explain had even made Sara feel better about the whole thing.

"Jeanette rarely works late, but we need to tell her and the other girls to be really careful. The neighborhood isn't what it used to be." Sara carried her glass with her into the living room. "After being away for a while, it's a lot easier to see the changes."

While Ellie had followed, she still hadn't said anything.

"I hope you're taking this seriously," Sara told her, then listened intently when she thought she heard her cell phone ringing upstairs.

"Hey, Sara?"

She looked back at Ellie.

"Your T-shirt's inside out," Ellie said with a mocking smile, and Sara felt the air leave her lungs. "Better go answer that. It's probably Robert."

8

SARA PACED BETWEEN two benches in Collect Pond Park with her cell at her ear. It was 8:00 p.m. in Rome, and Robert wasn't picking up. Sara would let it ring a few more times. He could be in the shower. Or something. She was getting sick of playing phone tag with him.

That they were already down to two calls a week—well, actually one now—wasn't nearly as upsetting as it should have been. It would be easy to think Dom had something to do with it, and if she hadn't experienced a few twinges of guilt over what happened two nights ago, she would've thought something was wrong with her. Especially since she hadn't even kissed another man since she and Robert had become exclusive.

They'd never actually talked about it, though, and while she hadn't been with anyone else, she honestly didn't know about Robert. While they'd still been in school, she'd say no. But since they'd been separated, she couldn't say with any certainty at all.

He'd skipped their last call. Each conversation started out well enough, always with him asking her how she was doing, only to quickly change to an in-depth report of Robert's *kick-ass* investigative reporting in Vatican City.

"Sara. Hey." He sounded breathless.

"Did I catch you at a bad time?"

"No, no. This is fine. I, uh, was just working and I got caught up."

"Still gathering facts about the conservatives?"

"Some, yeah, but I've gotten a couple of interviews with some more radical factions. This pope. I mean every day there's something new."

"I'll bet. You must be up to your ears in story ideas."

"That's so true. Like Angie says, this is the single most exciting time to be a journalist."

The sudden ache in her chest wasn't new either. Although it had nothing to do with whomever Angie was. Once upon a time, Sara would've done anything to be out in the world digging up hard news. "No wonder you skipped our last call."

"What? No." Robert's voice went up a couple octaves. "Angie had nothing to do with it."

"I meant that you were busy."

"Oh. Yeah." He cleared his throat. "That was my bad. I'm really sorry. I mean it, hon. I think about you all the time, but there's just been so much going on."

"Right. Can you hold on a second?"

"Yeah, sure." Robert's voice almost cut out on that last word.

She lowered her cell before calling out to her two charges. Beth and Bhodi were her neighbor's five- and seven-year-old kids, under Sara's care while Gail was busy getting out of jury duty at criminal court across the street. The kids were under strict orders to stick by Sara far away from the water feature, and to play nicely with their toys.

"Hey, kids, you're not supposed to be outside the big square, remember?"

Beth looked up and brought her doll back to the blanket that didn't do much to soften the concrete it covered. Instead of yelling at Bhodi, who was zooming his toy helicopter in circles above his head, Sara walked over, took his free hand and guided him back to the designated play area.

It was then she caught sight of Dom, standing almost directly across the park from her, staring at the bank of trees that lined the fence at Lafayette Street. The jolt to her system was magnified by the unbearably vivid memory of his mouth. She hadn't seen him since the night in her bedroom. But thoughts of him had been a recurring disruption.

He wrote furiously on a note pad, paused, shifted his gaze a bit, then wrote some more.

She couldn't decide if she wanted to wave and get his attention. The cell phone in her hand reminded her that Robert was still waiting. "You still there?"

"Who are Beth and Bhodi?"

"My friend's children. She has an appointment, so I'm babysitting."

"Maybe we should talk when you don't have such an important job to do."

Sara couldn't be sure if he'd actually sounded condescending or if she was the one imagining the tone. It had happened before, several times in fact, since he'd gone to Italy. "Who's Angie?"

"Oh. She's just—" His voice lowered. "She's another reporter."

"I'm sorry, could you repeat that?" Sara tried to keep a lid on her temper. "I didn't hear you." Guess she didn't have to wonder about the whole exclusive relationship thing. Or Angie. But that wasn't what made her angry.

After what had happened with Dom, she'd have some nerve if it did. But it wasn't just anger either. She was sad.

"She's a reporter," he repeated in a more normal voice.

"From?"

"Here. She's Italian."

Of course she was. Angie probably fit very well into the slot Sara had left. "How's your Italian? Any better?"

Robert replied with silence, so maybe she wasn't doing such a good job keeping her temper in check. Finally, he said, "Okay, you know what? Maybe it's time we had a talk."

"Can't right now. I've got an important job watching these kids."

She heard half a word, but she honestly couldn't have said what it was before she disconnected. She didn't particularly care about Angie, or anything Robert had to say at the moment. It should've been Sara out there digging deep, fighting to tell the truth. Human interest stories were fine, and Little Italy's history was particularly significant. But would she have cared enough to make it the subject of her thesis if she hadn't been beaten down in high school? And then held back again later by Robert's insecurities?

Competition was everywhere. She really should've told him to get over it.

She zeroed in on her charges, both safely in the zone, and then found Dom had moved from his original position, still writing in the notebook.

It wasn't a complete shock to see him in the area. Although it was now part of Chinatown, Collect Pond had played a major role in Little Italy during the early years. And Paladino & Sons did business all over the Lower East Side.

Her gaze swept up his long, lean body from his classic shoes to his well-tailored pants and jacket. Working, probably.

She hoped like hell he didn't have any interviews until his black eye faded. She'd hate to see it screw up his chance at a job he wanted. The thought made her feel ill. Dammit, where was Gail? Sara had been with the children for over an hour, when it should've been thirty minutes.

Her cell rang out a snippet from "Mad World" signaling an incoming text from Robert, which turned out to be very short and to the point.

Hey, I think we should see other people. Just for a while. Think about it?

"What a chicken sh—"

Beth tugged on Sara's jeans. "When's Mommy coming back?"

"Soon, honey." She smiled, imagining steam coming out of her ears at Robert's stunning cowardice. "Anytime now. In fact, get your dolly and your brother, and come walk with me so we'll be closer to where Mommy is supposed to meet us."

It didn't take but a minute to collect everything, and only two seconds to want to delete Robert's number from her contact list. Instead she let a whole bunch of juicy paybacks swirl through her brain. Stupid bastard. They'd talk eventually, even though she honestly didn't see the point.

And then her gaze caught on Dom again, and all thoughts of Robert died a suitable death. Her only decision now was whether or not to get his attention. Or maybe he'd seen her and chosen to ignore her. Well, she wouldn't know until she walked over there, closer to him and the Lafayette entrance. At least she had a good excuse.

His back was to her when she approached. So she had a few seconds to regulate her breathing. And decide how to handle seeing him after he'd seen her bare breasts. God.

"Oh, so, you're following me again?"

He jumped as if she'd slapped his butt, and then looked

at her through his sunglasses. "Sar— What? I've been here for almost an hour."

Her grin came easily, thank God. "Gotcha."

"Ha," he said, finally noticing that she was flanked by little kids. "Who are your friends?"

"This is Bhodi and Beth, and I'm watching them for my friend Gail. Who should be here anytime now."

He crouched down to their level. "Nice to meet you both," he said, and shook Bhodi's hand.

Beth put hers behind her back. "Are you a stranger?"

"No, he's a friend of mine," Sara said, a little surprised but happy to see the sweet way Dom interacted with the kids. "A nice man who probably knows your daddy. Ed McCoy."

"Yeah, sure. I played baseball with him in school. Your dad was a real good pitcher."

"Really?" Beth and Bhodi said at the same time.

"Yes, he was," Dom said, rising to his full height. "We won lots of games because of him. I bet he plays ball with you two."

Both kids nodded, and then they each turned to their toys.

A lot of things had changed in her world, but everyone knowing everyone who lived in their neighborhood? That would probably be true until the end of time. Or until the rest of her generation all moved away. The thought saddened her, even though she knew she'd soon be one of the defectors. "You have a job coming up here?"

He seemed confused for a moment. "No, just checking out a few things for a possible project. What about you? Working a lot?"

Having the kids with her was a stroke of luck. The moment could have been awkward, considering that she knew exactly how her breast fit in Dom's hand and what an excellent kisser—

"I'm sorry," she said, trying not to lose ground…or her mind. "You asked me something?"

A small smile lifted the corners of his mouth. "Have you been working a lot?"

"My folks are back, so I took a couple of days off to concentrate on my thesis. There's a senior residence in Brooklyn where I've found some folks whose families lived in the tenements."

"You haven't told me much about your dissertation."

"It's on the early history of Little Italy. Do you know the story of how this park came to be called Collect Pond?"

He shook his head. "If I ever heard it, I've forgotten."

"It used to be a forty-eight-acre natural spring and the Dutch called it *Kalck Hoek*, which got butchered somehow into Collect Pond. It became so polluted that the city ended up burying the whole area in landfill to build houses on."

"So not much has changed, then. Although I'm not so sure the city did us any favors with this renovation. It's barely a park, and that's a wading pool, not a pond."

"How's your eye?" she asked.

"Mending."

"May I see it?"

He slowly removed the sunglasses.

She held back a sigh. "Well, it's not horrible," she said, reaching over and brushing his eyebrow just above the cut.

The next second, his hand was around her wrist. "You never did finish telling me about the spring dance."

"I like to dance," Beth said, as she and her doll started to twirl. Sara wanted to hug the little one for giving her a reprieve, however brief.

"That's not dancing." Her brother stopped making helicopter noises long enough to give his sister a shove.

It was the perfect excuse to step back from Dom. She hadn't expected him to confront her like that, but she fully intended to tell him everything, no matter how silly it made her seem. "Stop it, Bhodi. No shoving." She inhaled and turned back to Dom. "I can't remember where I left off."

"You overheard me talking to my friends."

"Right." She nodded. "You told them that I'd be the last person you'd ever take to the dance. Because I wore braces and I was ugly and flat chested. And you had your pick of all the popular girls."

Dom's face reddened. "I said that? You heard me yourself?"

"Well, you and your gang were hanging out around the corner by the gym, so I didn't actually see you. But...it was you."

His jaw muscle flexed hard. "Anything else?"

She shook her head, glad he was wearing the sunglasses again, and wishing she had a pair.

"Oh, my God, Sara..."

She shrugged. "We were both kids, and I knew you didn't mean for me to hear. I was just, you know, a teenager. My feelings were hurt."

"Of course they were. I had no idea. I don't even remember saying that, but I'm appalled. I hate that I was such a dick."

She glanced at the kids, still bickering, not paying a lick of attention.

He caught her hand and lifted it to his lips. The kiss was gentle, more apologetic than words could have been.

She thought back to the hours she'd spent mentally obliterating him with scathing rejoinders, cutting him down to size in front of the whole school. That had been her inner scenario for years. Naturally that had changed over time, but to see him this revolted by his behavior, so repentant, touched a place deep inside her that had apparently needed some healing.

"I'm still mad at myself for bringing it up. It was so stupid."

"No, I'm glad." He didn't look glad. He looked devastated. "It needed to be said."

"Dom, please, you were fourteen. Don't give it another thought. Promise me."

"Mommy!"

Dom let go of her hand, and Sara looked out across the busy street to see Gail waving broadly at the crosswalk.

"I think she wants me to take the kids over there," Sara said. "Come on, guys. Let's go rescue Mommy."

The children jumped at the chance, literally, but she managed to capture their hands as she backed away.

Dom looked like a lost puppy watching her leave. Just as she was about to turn, he called out, "You going to the Easter feast?"

"Yeah," she said.

"You want to be my date?"

Again, a physical jolt. Like a sweet punch to the gut and just as confusing. She just laughed at his teasing, which she deserved, although, silly her, she wished he was serious.

As the light changed, the crowd at the corner forced her and the kids away from park, and back into the real world. The Easter feast was a tradition at the church their families had been going to forever. She'd never gone with a date.

When they reached Gail's side of the street, Sara wondered how much her friend had seen between her and Dom. If Gail asked, Sara had no idea what to tell her. They'd almost had sex the other night, but that didn't mean anything.

Another thought had Sara feeling slightly ill. Had Dom asked her to be his date out of guilt? Was that his way of doing penance?

9

DOM WALKED INTO the parish hall at the aging church the Paladinos had been going to for several generations.

No Sara in sight.

Not a surprise, it was still early. At his mother's request, he was here to help set up tables and chairs. He caught a glimpse of Tony coming out of the kitchen. Luca was undoubtedly around somewhere.

"Why are you just standing there?" Tony said. "Chairs."

Dom nodded. "You know, this place could use some help."

Tony frowned. "Meaning?"

"The kitchen is outdated, the playground is all concrete, I know the stained glass in the church needs repairs. The last thing they had done to the building was when we fixed the plumbing, and that was what, seven years ago?"

"Okay. Yeah. You should look into it. Talk it over with Dad. We could make a big difference here." Tony slapped him on the back. "Good thinking. Now go to work. It's going to get crowded in here real soon."

Dom started setting up chairs at the three long tables. Covered with white tablecloths, they already had place settings, water pitchers and wineglasses. In the back, closer to the kitchen, the big buffet table was also set up for the bounty of food the parishioners would bring.

Every time the door opened, Dom glanced over, hoping to see Sara. She'd said she was coming, but then she'd laughed at him when he'd asked her to be his date. What a dumbass he was. Asking her to come with him right after reminding her of his arrogant teens.

What he couldn't get over was how callous he'd been. Especially given his own sensitivity about being judged. His mom had once told him that he made everything look easy. His parents knew he'd worked hard to keep his grades up, to be his best at sports, but his casual demeanor made his classmates think all those accomplishments were effortless.

For him to have been cruel to Sara was unforgivable in his book. He still couldn't remember talking about her that way, but he believed her.

Damn, he wished he had her phone number.

Luca turned up, finally, to help him finish. He was two years older than Dom and they'd always had a good relationship. With half a stack of chairs left to put out, Dom said, "I got a question for you."

"Shoot."

"When I was a teenager, was I a dick?"

Luca laughed at him.

"I'm serious." Dom returned Mrs. Brivio's smile as she walked by with an antipasto tray. "I mean, yeah, I dated a lot of hot girls and hung out with the jocks sometimes, but—"

"Sometimes? You were always with those guys." Luca frowned. "Why are you bringing this up?"

"Someone told me I'd said something that just didn't sound like me. But clearly I have too high an opinion of myself."

"Nah, some of the guys you hung with were dicks, but not you. Tony or I would've slapped you upside the head."

"That's what I thought, but…" Dom shrugged. "Where's April?"

"Right there." Luca nodded toward the entrance, his face lighting up, just like it did every time his girlfriend was around.

April had just walked in, and behind her was Sara. With her parents. No Ellie in sight.

Dom abandoned his post instantly, ignoring Luca's, "Hey."

A bottleneck just inside the doorway slowed everyone down.

"April," he said, his eyes on Sara. "Luca's over there."

"What's with all the hats? Luca didn't say anything about wearing a hat. Oh, cute." April motioned to a teenager with blond hair who, along with most of the women in the hall, had followed the annual tradition of wearing a spring hat. "Where is he?"

Eyes only for Sara, Dom gestured behind him.

"You're going to have to be a little more specific," April said, which made Sara smile.

Dom snapped to. "Sorry. He's setting up chairs." He moved closer to the group, then sort of led them to the side so they wouldn't block the entrance. "I don't think you've met Sara Moretti and her parents, have you, April?"

"No, I haven't." She faced the trio with one of her big smiles. Her thick auburn hair was pulled into a twist of some kind, and her dress was light green. She was a knockout, and she'd made Luca happier than he'd ever been.

"April Branagan, meet Gio and Rose Moretti and their daughter Sara."

"I'm Luca's girlfriend," April said, nodding at them. "And after I check in with him, I'd love to chat if there's time. I'm still getting to know my way around the neighborhood. Darn, I wish he'd told me about the hat thing. You do this every year?"

"Yes," Gio said with a sigh. "Every year, and we go through the parade of hats fashion show for a week before. They say they want my opinion, but they never listen to me."

"Don't exaggerate, Gio," Mrs. M said, dismissing him with a wave of her hand.

Sara grinned. "Evidently the competition gets fiercer as the years go by. It feels more like the Kentucky Derby than a church gathering."

April laughed, but Dom only knew that because he heard her.

Sara looked beautiful in her white-and-pink sundress and her floppy brimmed hat.

Then April said she hoped to see everyone later and left to find Luca.

When Sara finally met his gaze, her eyes widened and she made sure he noticed her mother holding a covered platter.

Which he quickly took from her. The sucker was heavy. "I heard you guys were gallivanting all over Italy."

"It was a wonderful trip," Rose said at the exact same time her husband said, "It was exhausting."

Sara laughed, then touched Dom's elbow. "Why don't we get this to the kitchen? I'm going to see if I can help out."

"My mother should be here any minute," Dom told her parents. "I know she'll be anxious to hear all about your trip."

"And your father?" Mrs. M asked. "How is he doing?"

"He's doing great. He'll be here, too."

Sara hadn't even waited for him and was moving fast in her high-heeled sandals.

"Hey, I was hoping to see you at the restaurant last night," he said, after catching up to her. "Ellie didn't seem too happy with me."

"It's not you. Trust me. You walk on water. She's reasonably certain that I, however, am the devil incarnate, out to steal you from under her very nose."

Dom laughed. "You're kidding, right?"

Sara stared at him in surprise. "Come on," she said. "You must know she has a crush on you."

"Because she gives me free sodas?"

"Oh, please." Sara studied his face long enough for him to get a little edgy. "For God's sake, Dominic."

"I'm twenty-eight. What is she, seventeen?"

"And you think that matters? Did you ever have a crush on a teacher?"

Biology. Sophomore year. Mrs. Walker. With legs that went on forever. "Point taken."

"By the way, your eye looks good. It's barely discolored. Doesn't hurt, does it?"

"Only when no one kisses it." He held back a laugh when her eyes rounded to the size of pizzas, and he leaned toward her.

"You're insane," she muttered, swatting at him and glancing around. "Get away from me."

She got her wish when Mr. Albrogetti came through on his wheelchair. They parted in the small area between tables, giving Dom time to think about what she'd told him. He supposed on some level he knew Ellie was overly friendly, though most girls her age were. But Ellie being Sara's sister—that wasn't good.

"She's going to be here in a little while." Sara looked

back over the growing crowd and didn't seem anxious to meet his eyes again. "So, um, did you bring a date?"

He snorted. "Well, since the woman I wanted to bring blew me off, no, I don't have one."

Sara blinked at him. "Do you mean—" She bit her lip, and there was that shy streak again. "I thought you were teasing."

Mrs. Martinelli and her brood of troublemakers—all under seventeen and looking like professional linebackers— were bearing down on them. Dom pulled Sara out of the path to the kitchen and closer to him. "I have a little crush on you, Sara Moretti," he whispered in her ear. "Didn't you get that?"

SARA STARED AT HIM, not sure what to think. If this was his guilt talking, she swore on all that was holy, she'd die a thousand deaths. But how would she know? Unless she asked him, which wasn't something she thought she could do. Maybe.

They'd picked the worst possible spot to have their conversation. It was already packed with more people than code allowed. Just inside the kitchen, four different ovens, each of them ancient, were in use, the generous counters stacked with everything from baked hams to trays of cookies.

The platter was whisked away before they could blink, and the two of them were shooed out again, straight into the path of a woman Sara hadn't seen in years.

"Sarafina Moretti," the older woman said. She was dressed, like most of the women in the room, in her Easter finery.

"Mrs. Jacometti, how nice to see you."

"I heard you were in town. Regina told me you had a big interview with her and that no-good husband of hers."

Dom hid his grin, but Sara laughed. She'd known the

sisters since she'd sold them Girl Scout cookies. They were always arguing and were both married to men who were so alike it was scary.

"Actually, I was hoping I could talk with you and Mr. Jacometti about when his family first arrived in the country."

"What about my family, because whatever Regina said is completely wrong. She thinks she remembers, but she doesn't. Lousy memory. You ask me, she should get it checked, but will she listen? Never."

"Well, I look forward to it. I'll give you a call after the holiday?"

"Good. Yes. Happy Easter."

When Sara turned back to Dom, he was looking at his mother, who was waving him over to her and Mr. Paladino's table near the wall. "Dinner's about to start," she said. "Sara, you, too." She pointed to the chairs opposite them. "Your parents are sitting here."

Dom turned back to her and leaned in. She felt certain he was about to kiss her, but he stopped. Right along with her heart. Enough people had already seen them together. They barely had to do anything more than talk three seconds too long for rumors to start flying.

"Is that going to be a problem?" Dom asked, glancing at the table.

"Why?"

"Won't Ellie be sitting with your parents?"

"Oh, crap." Sara rubbed her temple. Ellie had been behaving perfectly when the family was together. She'd saved her snarky remarks for Sara.

Before she could think what to do next, her mother was behind her, literally pushing her toward the empty seats.

"Wait, what about Ellie?"

"She's with her friends."

Dom caught her eye and gave her a sympathetic look

before he turned back to walk around the table, almost lost in the sea of bobbing feathers and fruit that bedecked Easter hats of every color.

Sara was practically shoved into her seat, the one directly across from Dom's. Her mother sat opposite Theresa Paladino, and her father faced Joe with a weary nod as he settled himself in the plastic chair. The whole setup was eerily reminiscent of her adolescence, the era of braces and double-A bras and hiding behind her hair.

And the disaster that had come from her crush on Dom.

"You look wonderful, Rose," Theresa said. "The trip to the old country has made you look ten years younger."

"Nonsense. But you look terrific and, Joseph, you'd never know you had a moment's trouble. What a blessing to be here with all our children."

Joe nodded, and Sara couldn't even pretend that her mother and Dom's weren't both looking as if they'd been planning this reunion since the moment they first met. She kept having to smile back at Theresa, who would wiggle her eyebrows, then bob her head toward Dom. It was like something out of a cartoon.

Her own mother was no better, bringing Dom into a conversation about Theresa's hat, of all things.

"You must have helped her pick it out," Rose said.

Sara hid her laugh behind a fake cough, unable to meet Dom's eyes.

Rose elbowed her husband. "Doesn't Dominic have good taste?"

"I'm sure he does," Gio said. "Where's the wine?"

"It's too soon for the wine."

"Not if you're going to talk about hats."

Theresa rolled her eyes, then caught Sara, who should have known better than to do anything but stare at her plate. "Sarafina, we've all missed you. So nice you came home after college. You know, Dom has also graduated. A bachelor's degree and two master degrees. Tell her, Dom."

"She knows, Ma."

"But do her parents?"

"I'm positive her parents don't care about my degrees."

"What? Of course we do," Rose said. "Tell him, Gio."

"We care," Gio said, having gotten his hands on a bottle of wine which he was busy uncorking.

"Well, look at that," Dom said, standing up, shocking Sara, and everyone else who'd been eavesdropping, which must have been half the parish. "Tony and Catherine are sitting all by themselves. Sara, you haven't met Catherine yet, right? She's engaged to Tony. You'll like her."

Sara practically leaped up. "You're right. I haven't met her. I've been meaning to." She scooted her chair in. "We'll be back in a minute," then she was walking as fast as she could, although not as quickly as Dom.

Once they were a safe distance away, Dom touched her arm. "You okay?" he asked. The way he looked at her was more concerned than annoyed. Which made her chest tighten. The last thing on earth she wanted was to remind him of the last time their moms had played matchmakers.

"I'm fine," she said, keeping her voice light as a breeze. "I'm just hoping Father Michael makes his address soon."

"Oh, he will. Unfortunately, it won't stop them from talking. And plotting. God, they all need hobbies."

Before they reached Tony and Catherine, who hadn't even taken seats yet, raised voices coming from the kitchen had them turning their heads. Regina stormed out, grumbling about her crazy sister and their mother's special recipe. They didn't calm down until Father Michael stepped in and refereed.

Saddest thing of all was the evening had just begun.

10

BY THE TIME the longest meal he'd ever suffered through was over, Dom felt like going to the gym just so he could punch something. Sara had gone to the kitchen to offer her help cleaning up. Dom, who hoped he didn't feel quite so full by the time he had to do any heavy lifting in the hall, had found Henry Randal, his old high school coach, talking to Mike Cho and Aiden Gallagher, both teammates back in the day.

"Did I just hear you mention retirement?" Dom asked, guessing Randal was in his early forties by now.

"That's right. These damn kids today spend too much time playing with their cell phones instead of practicing or keeping in shape."

Aiden laughed. "I don't recall you having any problem kicking a few asses."

"And you guys listened after that. Not these kids today, they don't listen to nobody. Neither do their crybaby parents."

Dom exchanged looks with Aiden and Mike. Many of those parents were in the hall at the moment. Not that Randal seemed to care because he wasn't watching his tone or keeping his voice down. On top of that, Dom thought he noticed the coach slur the last two words, but then there'd been a hell of a lot of wine served.

Mike and Aiden steered the conversation to past victories and bad calls from stupid referees. Dom managed a laugh here and there, but he was distracted by his lookout for Sara, and he regretted joining the group. He wasn't crazy about the coach's language with so many kids nearby. Aiden and Mike seemed uncomfortable, too.

It didn't help that even though all the windows were open, the number of people in the large hall made the place swelter, and he longed to take Sara for a walk to cool off. Then, if he was lucky, turn up the heat in a whole different way.

"Look out," Mike said, staring past Dom's left shoulder. "Here comes trouble."

Dom turned to find Sara, hat off, her beautiful hair pinned up with just a few tendrils floating around her face and neck. She smiled, and he instantly felt better.

"Who's that?" Coach asked.

"That's Sara." Dom motioned her over, belatedly realizing he should've used the excuse to escape. "You remember her from Loyola, right?" he said, stepping aside to include her in the group.

Coach gave her a look that was a little too intense. "You can't be the one who wrote for the school paper?"

She tilted her head in that way she had, and he could tell she didn't remember Coach Randal. Why would she?

"Yeah, that's right," Dom said. "We used to go to her family's pizzeria after games sometimes. You know Moretti's?"

"Right." Coach nodded. "So you're still slinging pizza?"

Dom blinked, not sure he liked the way Coach said that. "She's helping out her folks while she completes her master's thesis."

"Oh?"

Sara just smiled gracefully and said, "Yes, I'm getting my masters in journalism."

"Interesting." Randal nodded. "So I hope you learned a good lesson, then."

She frowned. "Meaning?"

So did Dom. "What are you talking about?"

"I probably did you a big favor," Coach said, nodding and looking pleased with himself. "Principal Hayes thought I went too far, but I did what I had to do. And look how well everything turned out." His gaze ran briefly down her body.

Sara stiffened. More confused than ever, and not liking the way Randal looked at her, Dom wasn't about to let this shit ride. He needed to know what was going on, and right now.

He felt her hand on his arm. "Can I steal you away for a minute?" she asked, her voice tighter than it should have been.

Both Mike and Aiden seemed as weirded out as Dom, but Coach just looked smug. For a guy he'd respected since his first year at Loyola, Randal was acting like a real asshole.

"Sure." Dom let Sara lead him away by the arm. But as soon as they were out of earshot, he stopped and she let go. "What was he talking about?"

"I thought it was you," she said. "All these years. Oh, my God."

"Thought what was me?"

"That horrible piece I wrote. I got taken off the paper. The principal couldn't do anything about it. There'd been a complaint to the school board that I'd besmirched you and the athletics program, and everyone wanted me gone."

"You thought I'd complained to the school board?"

"You had every reason to."

"I would never have done that. I was mad, sure. But I only ever spoke about it to my teammates. And Coach."

"Well, I suppose he had a right, as well."

"That's why you weren't editor your senior year," he said, mostly to himself, feeling his anger rise at the audacity of his supposed mentor. He'd never said a word to Dom about a complaint. But what had him truly steamed was the way he'd just treated Sara. Condescending bastard. He turned back, ready to tell his ex-coach exactly what he could do with his attitude.

"Dom, wait."

"I'll be right back."

Sara grabbed his arm. "Please. It doesn't matter."

"Of course it matters. The way he—"

"It's been ten years. Nothing's going to change the past. And I don't give a damn what he thinks of me."

"I do."

"Please don't." Her grip on his arm tightened when he tried to pull away. "How about we get out of here?"

"What?" He locked gazes with Sara, aware that everyone standing around them was probably watching. "Now?"

She nodded. "Please."

"I'm supposed to—"

"I'm sure there are enough volunteers to straighten up."

He saw the worried crease between her brows, probably afraid he'd do something rash. Like punch Randal in his goddamn nose. Dom hoped he had more self-restraint than that, but he was pretty damn steamed. "You know what? Let's go. I know a nice place around the corner where we can get a drink in peace."

He started to take her hand but she moved it away. Could've been a coincidence. If it wasn't, he didn't blame her. People around here read too much into every damn thing.

"You realize everyone's going to see we're leaving together," Sara said, halfway to the door.

"Do you care?"

"Not really, but—"

"Oh, shit." He stopped. "Ellie." How could he have forgotten? Because he still wanted to lay Coach flat, that's how.

"She's already guessed we're a little bit more than friends."

"Won't this make things worse?"

"If it does, I'll work it out." She started for the exit and he stayed with her. "Honestly, it's too late anyway. The gossip probably started the moment our moms began behaving like five-year-olds. Can you believe those two?"

He laughed, feeling some of his tension ease.

"Well, as far as I'm concerned, they can be the ones who field the rumors and nosy questions."

"The minute we get to the bar, we'll drink to that."

"Agreed. It'll be their problem. Because, frankly, it's only going to get worse."

"Not necessarily."

"It will if I don't make it home tonight."

He stopped right in the doorway. "Really?"

"Maybe." She met his eyes with just the tiniest bit of shyness. "That is, if you don't have any objections."

"Oh, hell. Not a single one," he said, taking her by the arm and hurrying them outside.

AT SARA'S INSISTENCE they ended up at the Mulberry Street Bar first. Dom was still so pissed at his ex-coach that she thought it was a good idea for him to have a drink and cool down. What she didn't tell him was that she needed a drink just as much, if not more.

Everything had happened so fast, and yes, she really wanted to go home with him, but she was nervous. About Ellie, about her parents, Dom's parents... Even if they hadn't seen them leave together—after all, the hall was ridiculously crowded—there was a very good chance they'd hear about it.

Mostly, though, she was nervous about what was going to happen after they got to his apartment.

She hadn't been with a lot of men before, and after last night's stilted conversation with Robert that made it clear they were done, she was free to do as she wished. But the fact that it was Dom was intimidating.

She took a big sip of her Bushmills on the rocks, letting the heat slide all the way down before she set her glass on the small table. That's when she noticed Dom watching her. Probably because she'd been nibbling on her lip. Stupid nervous habit.

"I can't imagine how much you must've hated me," Dom said. "Thinking I'd gotten you kicked off the paper."

Sara inhaled. "There were moments," she admitted. "But then I'd remember I was the one who caused all the trouble in the first place."

"I don't know about that..." he said, staring at his snifter of brandy. "Not after what you'd heard come out of my mouth." He swore under his breath and tossed the amber liquid back with a single gulp.

Well, this wasn't going as planned. "Come on." Sara touched his arm. "You were fourteen. I doubt anyone is particularly proud of their teenage years. Including me." She sighed. "Obviously."

A faint smile curved his mouth. "The whole thing

started before you wrote that article. Guess it's kind of what came first, the chicken or the egg."

"Okay, if you want to get that technical, then it's our mothers' fault."

They both laughed, which seemed to relax Dom a little.

The waitress came by, but neither of them was ready for another drink. Sara still had half of her whiskey. She sure wouldn't mind a second one before they left for his apartment, though.

"I've been wondering about something," Dom said. "I know your thesis is on the history of Little Italy, and I'm assuming you're taking more of a human interest type angle. Am I in the right ballpark?"

Sara nodded, pretty sure she knew what he was going to say.

"I think it's great. We've all heard the stories about our ancestors coming over but who knows what's fact or fiction? But I gotta say I'm a little surprised you didn't go after something meatier."

"Only a little surprised?"

"Hey, I'm not saying it isn't an interesting topic. I just keep remembering the day you took on the faculty—"

"I know exactly what you're saying." She took another sip. "I've been asking myself the same question lately." And she knew part of the answer, but it wasn't something she was willing to share.

Dom sat patiently waiting, then moved his hand to cover hers. "We don't have to talk about this."

Sara shook her head. "It isn't any one particular reason. I made an emotional decision to write that op-ed before thinking it through. I was a hormonal kid, so who knows why I did it. So in a way, Randal wasn't wrong—I did learn a valuable lesson."

Dom's jaw clenched and she instantly regretted mentioning the coach. "I don't care what led him to do it—he had no right filing a formal complaint."

She turned her hand over so their palms pressed together. "Actually, he did since I attacked the athletic program."

"Everyone—parents, teachers, the school board, they all could've read what you wrote for themselves. But Randal used my name, didn't he?"

She picked up her glass but it was empty.

Dom signaled the waitress.

"I was shy," Sara said, shrugging. "I stepped over the line to make my mark, first questioning the faculty, which I'm not at all ashamed of, but then I came out with that awful piece, which was completely my fault. So of course all I wanted to do was crawl back into my shell."

They remained quiet for a while, their palms touching, and their fingers semientwined. Until the waitress arrived with the drinks. They pulled apart to make room for her glass and his snifter.

Sara missed his touch. The second whiskey was a poor substitute. Although focusing on the heady taste helped take the edge off when he refused to look away.

"Being removed as editor must've hurt your chances at a college journalism program," Dom said.

"You know what? Can we not talk about it?" she asked, and realized she should've lied, just said no. Except Dom was too smart for that.

"No problem," he said, giving her a warm a smile. "We don't have to talk about anything at all."

He picked up the snifter, swirled the brandy, then downed half of it. He was getting pretty mellow. It was times like these that Sara really appreciated living in a city with so many cabs.

The waitress stopped briefly, just to leave a check, startling Sara, because she hadn't seen Dom ask for it.

Leaning forward he touched her cheek, and let an escaped tendril of hair curl around his finger. "Are you ready?" he asked, his voice pitched low.

"I am." She hoped.

11

STILL FEELING A tiny bit nervous and only slightly buzzed, Sara crossed the nicely decorated lobby in Dom's building. He kept his arm around her as he guided her past the normal-sized elevator to a much-smaller one in the corner.

"So, this is private?" she asked as she stepped inside. "No one else can use it?"

Dom nodded, a smile tugging at his mouth as he used a key, and graciously refrained from pointing out that he'd already explained the setup. Twice.

He was facing Sara as the elevator climbed to his unit on the eighth floor. Knowing what was to come made her skin tingle, her breathing quick and sharp, and she had to squeeze her thighs together just from staring into his dark, seductive eyes. "That means, when the door opens, we'll be in your…apartment?"

"Yep."

"So it isn't called something different because it's the whole floor?"

"Not that I know of."

Sara walked across the small car, which admittedly only took three steps. "So there shouldn't be any problem with me doing this," she said and unfastened the top button of his shirt.

"None at all," he said, his voice a sexy growl, raising her already high temperature.

She took her time with the second button, his warm breath, still sweet with brandy, skimming across her cheek.

Another button. A moment to spread his shirt apart that little bit more. A soft sigh across his tanned skin.

He touched her then, his hands on the back of her thighs, just underneath the hem of her dress. Luckily, she'd worn nice underwear. Nothing fancy. She didn't own anything exotic, or even exciting, unless he considered bikini panties a thrill.

The slight tremor in his palms as they inched higher suggested he might.

She undid the next button.

His breathing changed. Not as if he'd been running long-distance or anything, but it was noticeable. Feeling daring, she leaned forward and licked a strip up his throat to the tip of his lifted chin.

A second later he moved his hands so his fingers could slip beneath the waistband of her panties. When he grasped each of her cheeks in his big hands, her breath caught. His squeeze wasn't altogether gentle, which turned up the heat again. And when he lifted her straight up against his body, she gasped and wrapped her arms around his neck, her moan echoing loudly in that little box.

The elevator doors parted. Dom stepped away from the wall, still holding her up with his hands cupping her butt. She wrapped her legs around him and continued her exploration of his neck.

"You want a tour of the place?" he said, his voice still raspy and moving quickly as if he was on a mission.

"Sure," she said, nipping the tender skin that covered his jugular.

"Windows, living room, walls," he said, right before he groaned. When he could speak again, he added, "Bathroom, bedroom."

"It's gorgeous," she said, though she hadn't actually seen anything.

"Yeah. Ready?"

"For?"

"Oh, so much."

She felt him bump against what she knew had to be the mattress—her cue to release him from the press of her thighs. A moment later, he managed to set her down at the edge of the bed, her feet firmly on the floor even though she felt as though she were floating in the clouds.

This was the boy she'd dreamed about, the amazing man he'd turned into. And that was him, looking at her as if she was the most desirable woman on the planet.

If it turned out to be a dream, she'd be crushed.

"God, you're gorgeous," he said, finishing the job with his buttons. "In every way."

She kicked her heels away and lifted up enough to slip her panties off and tug her sundress up above her waist.

"You're trying to kill me," Dom muttered, running a gaze over her.

She felt the heat of a blush on her cheeks. Her two whiskeys had given her more than enough courage. She'd always been shy about her body. First because, well, Catholic school, but also because she'd been embarrassed by most everything as a young girl. Even when she went off to college, she'd been with only two other men besides Robert, and she'd made sure the lights were off and she was under the covers before she'd stripped bare.

YOUR PARTICIPATION IS REQUESTED!

Dear Reader,

Since you are a lover of our books – we would like to get to know you!

Inside you will find a short Reader's Survey. Sharing your answers with us will help our editorial staff understand who you are and what activities you enjoy.

To thank you for your participation, we would like to send you 2 books and 2 gifts – **ABSOLUTELY FREE!**

Enjoy your gifts with our appreciation,

Pam Powers

SEE INSIDE FOR READER'S SURVEY

For Your Reading Pleasure...

We'll send you 2 books and 2 gifts
ABSOLUTELY FREE
just for completing our Reader's Survey!

YOUR READER'S SURVEY
"THANK YOU" FREE GIFTS INCLUDE:
▶ 2 FREE books

▶ 2 lovely surprise gifts

PLEASE FILL IN THE CIRCLES COMPLETELY TO RESPOND

1) What type of fiction books do you enjoy reading? (Check all that apply)
- ○ Suspense/Thrillers
- ○ Action/Adventure
- ○ Modern-day Romances
- ○ Historical Romance
- ○ Humor
- ○ Paranormal Romance

2) What attracted you most to the last fiction book you purchased on impulse?
- ○ The Title
- ○ The Cover
- ○ The Author
- ○ The Story

3) What is usually the greatest influencer when you <u>plan</u> to buy a book?
- ○ Advertising
- ○ Referral
- ○ Book Review

4) How often do you access the internet?
- ○ Daily ○ Weekly ○ Monthly ○ Rarely or never

5) How many NEW paperback fiction novels have you purchased in the past 3 months?
- ○ 0 - 2
- ○ 3 - 6
- ○ 7 or more

YES! I have completed the Reader's Survey. Please send me the 2 FREE books and 2 FREE gifts (gifts are worth about $10 retail) for which I qualify. I understand that I am under no obligation to purchase any books, as explained on the back of this card.

150/350 HDL GLNY

FIRST NAME

LAST NAME

ADDRESS

APT.#

CITY

STATE/PROV.

ZIP/POSTAL CODE

READER SERVICE—Here's how it works:

Accepting your 2 free Harlequin® Blaze® books and 2 free gifts (gifts valued at approximately $10.00) places you under no obligation to buy anything. You may keep the books and gifts and return the shipping statement marked "cancel." If you do not cancel, about a month later we'll send you 4 additional books and bill you just $4.99 each in the U.S. or $5.46 each in Canada. That is a savings of at least 13% off the cover price. It's quite a bargain! Shipping and handling is just 50¢ per book in the U.S. and 75¢ per book in Canada.* You may cancel at any time, but if you choose to continue, every month we'll send you 4 more books, which you may either purchase at the discount price plus shipping and handling or return to us and cancel your subscription. *Terms and prices subject to change without notice. Prices do not include applicable taxes. Sales tax applicable in N.Y. Canadian residents will be charged applicable taxes. Offer not valid in Quebec. Books received may not be as shown. All orders subject to approval. Credit or debit balances in a customer's account(s) may be offset by any other outstanding balance owed by or to the customer. Please allow 4 to 6 weeks for delivery. Offer available while quantities last.

▲ If offer card is missing write to: Reader Service, P.O. Box 1867, Buffalo, NY 14240-1867 or visit www.ReaderService.com ▲

BUSINESS REPLY MAIL
FIRST-CLASS MAIL   PERMIT NO. 717   BUFFALO, NY

POSTAGE WILL BE PAID BY ADDRESSEE

READER SERVICE
PO BOX 1867
BUFFALO NY 14240-9952

NO POSTAGE
NECESSARY
IF MAILED
IN THE
UNITED STATES

Dom didn't even have his pants off yet, and she was half-naked.

The bulge at his fly had to be uncomfortable. A frisson shot up her spine, a first for her. She'd only read about the sensation. She had a feeling it wouldn't be the only first she'd experience tonight.

He winced as he pressed his hand over his erection, but then he got busy with his belt, button and zipper, which he pulled down very gingerly.

"Sara, Sara, Sara…what are you doing to me?" he said teasingly.

She stared, transfixed, as he lowered his dress pants, revealing the outline of his erection vivid in his tight navy boxer briefs. There was a damp spot high up that made her blush deepen.

He tossed aside his clothes, almost naked now, except for his briefs, and she took advantage of the moment and looked at the whole of him. No one in her real life had ever been as ripped. He wasn't overly muscled, but what was there was perfectly defined from his pecs to his abs, all the way down to his thighs and calves.

Martial arts, huh? She wished she'd worked out more. And that she hadn't gained those three pounds since she'd started working at the parlor.

All thoughts left her as he lowered his underwear. She still had her dress half-on. No way was she missing a second of this unveiling, though. He was—

"I can't stand this much longer," he said, his voice tight, as if something were squeezing his neck. The second his boxers had cleared his erection, he let them fall, turned to open his bedside drawer and grabbed a few condoms, leaving them all on the table. When he sat down, he put his arm around her. "Everything okay?"

She tried to take in a deep breath, but her body wasn't

having it. A few moments ago she'd been ready to swing from the chandeliers, and now she felt as nervous as a virgin on her wedding night.

"I don't know why I'm being so—weird all of a sudden."

"We can take this as slowly as you want."

She kind of snorted, which didn't help things. "Uh, it looks like slow is the last thing you need."

"I'll be fine." He smiled, rubbing her back, taking his time, letting her keep the bottom of her stupid dress bunched in her stupid hands.

When he kissed her, it was gentle. Sweet. She'd wanted things to be wild, untamed. This fantasy was turning into a soap opera.

His hand cupped the back of her neck, and with the tip of his tongue he brushed the seam between her lips.

Something clicked and she kissed him back, letting everything else go. Right this moment, this kiss, his tongue, the taste of him, the way he breathed, was all that existed.

He didn't hurry her or make her feel anything but special. His low moan made that thrill slip down her back again, and she found herself squeezing her internal muscles, all kinds of sensations wakening once more.

When she touched him, it helped her relax even more. He might be the most handsome man she'd ever been with, but he was also just Dom. The guy picking pineapple chunks off his pizza as if they'd kill him, who'd come to her aid even after she'd been a jerk.

He wasn't the boy of her memories, or the man she'd imagined. He was so much better. So much more real.

When he ran his hand down her back, she didn't want her dress on anymore. Pulling back from his kiss, her heart skipped a beat when he chased her mouth before he realized what she was doing.

She lifted her dress up and over her head, tossing it aside, then reached behind to unhook her decidedly plain bra, and let the shoulder straps fall.

With his pupils blown wide, he looked close to desperate, but he didn't rush her. His breathing quickened and he licked his lips, but he kept his hands to himself.

That had to stop.

After straightening her back, the bra came off, and there, it was done. She was as naked as he was, and while his erection was hard to miss, so were her very pebbled nipples, so they were even. Kind of.

"I want to touch you everywhere." Lifting his right hand, he hovered between her shoulder and her breast, as if he didn't know where to begin.

Or maybe he was waiting for her.

Taking his hand, she placed it so her nipple hit the center of his palm. "How's that for starters?"

He just groaned, his eyelids fluttering as he took her mouth once again.

They kissed and explored each other, reaching what they could. The second he sucked her nipple into his mouth, she struggled to catch her breath. He knew just how hard to suck, just how much pressure to use as he thumbed her other nipple. But when she touched his thick, hot penis, he stopped her.

"Wait," he said, arching back. "I don't want this over before we've begun."

"What do you mean? We began in the elevator. I think I've tortured you enough by now, don't you?"

His hoarse laugh against the side of her neck almost threw her off track. "This isn't torture," he whispered, his warm breath forging a trail from her ear to her shoulder. Back up to her throat. Down to her left breast. The tip of his tongue barely grazed her nipple.

Sara gasped. "Oh. This—" She drew in a shaky breath. "This is definitely torture."

He glanced up and gave her a wicked smile. "But the good kind, right?"

"Okay," she said, leaning over him until she could reach a condom on the bedside table. "You're going to put this on while I get more comfortable."

He stared at her for a long moment, one dark brow lifted in question.

"Now," she said, and hid a grin when he snatched the packet as if it were a lifeline.

It was exciting, taking the lead like that. She had no problem being assertive in every other area of her life, but with men, it hadn't worked that way. This felt liberating. Sexy as hell.

She started to pull her legs up on the mattress, but realized she'd rather have the linens pulled down, especially the comforter. He'd already stood to sheathe himself, so she hurried around to the other side of the bed.

Together, they got the bedding managed, and then she laid herself out, her heart beating like a rabbit's and her insides all aflutter.

"What's that smile for?" he asked, dipping the mattress with his knees.

"Nothing."

He leaned over and took a kiss that chased away any possible shred of doubt. "I want you," he said, his lips so close they almost brushed hers. "You, Sarafina Moretti. From the inside out and all around."

She had no idea what that meant. And with her heart pummeling her chest, she couldn't possibly care less.

He shifted, slipping his right knee between her thighs, pushing them gently apart. "I was prepared to wait as long as I had to."

She opened herself to him until he was resting on his hands, looking down into her eyes. "I think we've both waited long enough," she whispered.

Keeping his gaze on her, he moved his right hand down and slipped two fingers just inside her, stroking her slowly, pausing at her sensitive clit.

She trembled, fighting to keep her eyes open. When she lifted her hips, Dom swore. His curse made her grin, and she ran a hand down his back, the other up the arm that held him so steady. God, she was so turned on by his muscles, his strength. He was steel beneath hot flesh.

Her touch spurred him on, his thumb at her clit now, circling, circling. Her own moans sounded distant as the pressure inside soared, the blood rushing past her ears in the prelude to an orgasm.

So fast. She'd never gotten there so quickly, not with help, not by herself. But the foreplay truly had started even before they'd stepped into the elevator. The moment she'd seen his fury over his ex-coach.

"Come on," he whispered, his quiet ferocity ratcheting up the tension in her body.

When she reached between them, she could only touch the end of his cock. He froze, trembling.

"Should I stop?"

He nodded, a drop of sweat falling to the pillow. "I want to see you," he said, barely moving his jaw. With his thumb hitting her exactly at the right place, with the perfect pressure, she couldn't help pushing up as the climax turned from promise to unstoppable.

"Yes," she said, gripping his arm, scrabbling at the sheet next to her hip. "Yes, yes." Then it hit. A jerk and release that spread from her toes all the way up until she was somewhere else. Not floating, but flying.

The next thing she felt, outside of her own pleasure, was

the sensation of him entering her. Thrusting in carefully until she pushed back hard.

That unleashed the floodgate and, with both hands holding him steady now, he was all strength and need, every muscle in his body straining as he took what he wanted, what she wanted him to have.

Shudders swept through her, as if every nerve was on full alert, the sensations sharp, wonderful, electric.

"Sara," he said, his voice breaking. "Oh—" His eyes widened as if struck by complete surprise, then his head reared back as he stilled, pulsing inside, quivering and gritting his teeth to hold back a cry.

Another aftershock jerked them both.

When he started breathing again, he stayed where he was, pushed inside her to the brink, studying her face as if she'd become someone new. "You," he said, right before he kissed her.

Not the smoothest kiss she'd ever had—they were both too breathless—but maybe the best.

"Yeah," she said, when they broke apart. "You."

He grinned, then flopped to her side, his head next to hers, his chest rising and falling even more quickly than her own.

She stared at the ceiling, her thoughts a jumble.

Then his hand found hers and he threaded their fingers until they were perfectly entwined.

12

DOM SQUEEZED SARA'S HAND, still overwhelmed by what had just happened. Somehow, it had gotten late. Really late, and they were still naked, and he needed to get cleaned up, and they could both use a drink, but he didn't want to move. Not because he was lazy...

Because he was so content.

He turned his head to ask Sara if she was chilly, looked straight into her soft hazel eyes and said, "So what are we doing?"

Sara's little gasp came as a surprise. "What do you mean?"

"I mean, you and Ellie aren't speaking, your folks must know you left with me, but I'm pretty sure they're not thrilled that you haven't gone home yet. In fact, a lot of people who saw us leave together probably kept a close eye to see if we showed up back at the hall, and I don't want you to regret any of this."

"Do you?"

"Me? Hell, no." He let go of her hand, but only to turn on his side so he could watch her more easily. The room was dark, but he could see her by the light of the streetlamps coming in through the linen sheers. "I want to go out with you again. But I know your family and this neighborhood. Since college I haven't dated all that much, but I've heard my bachelor days have been greatly exaggerated, and that doesn't seem to matter to anyone but me."

"Oh, tell me. I haven't heard any of the juicy stuff yet."

Not at all sure if she was kidding, he studied her in the dim light, trying to find the answer in her normally expressive face. Then he saw her lips start to curve. "Keep it up and I'll lock you in here for a week."

Sara burst out laughing. "If you're trying to discourage me, it's not working."

He loved her laugh, her smile and the sound of her voice, even when she lost her temper. "Discourage you from what?" he asked, touching her petal-soft cheek, rubbing it lightly with his thumb.

"Yes, I want to see you again, and no, I don't care what people think." She turned her head so she could stare at the ceiling. Or perhaps so she wouldn't have to look at him. "So, we're sex buddies." She paused and slanted him a quick glance. "Right? Which is fine. I don't want to put you on the spot or anything." Something on the ceiling sure fascinated her. "I mean, you know I'm only planning to be here until my thesis is finished, and you, well, you're interviewing and moving on with your life."

His gaze moved down her body as she turned to face him again. So beautiful. Naked in the murky light, she seemed more like a dream than the very real woman he knew her to be. "Sex buddies," he murmured.

"You know, friends with benefits," she said, her tone casual, although he didn't miss the way she bit down on her lower lip.

Sex buddies.

Friends with benefits.

Jesus. He wasn't saying that at all. "In Little Italy?"

"I'm not suggesting we broadcast it. No one would know, not even our parents. Or Ellie."

"And that arrangement would be all right with you?"

"Well…" She lifted a shoulder. "Yes."

Dom didn't understand why it pissed him off. He should be thrilled. What wasn't to like about an arrangement like that? Actually, it was right up his alley.

"I'm just saying I don't expect you to treat it like we're dating or anything."

"Well, too damn bad, because that's not all right with me," he said, and she stared at him, eyes wide, her confusion obvious even in the dim light. In many ways she was so observant, but he guessed he'd have to spell it out for her. "Dammit, Sara Moretti, will you have dinner with me tomorrow night?"

She blinked and her face changed. Her smile broadened into something real. "Depends," she said. "Where?"

Giving a casual shrug, he thought about it for a second. "I thought we could go for a slice at Lombardi's."

She slugged him in the shoulder.

"Ow. That hurt."

"You deserved it. Never say that name in the presence of a Moretti. Ever."

"So when I pick you up tomorrow evening, I shouldn't mention it to your father?"

She blew out a breath. "Oh, boy. You're really going to do that? You know, pick me up?"

"Why? Are you ashamed to go out with me?"

"Oh, shut up."

"What?"

"You're the last man in all of Manhattan that should be fishing for compliments."

"That's not— Okay, I see this conversation is going downhill." He gave her a quick kiss and then rolled off the bed. "Think about where you'd like to go while I excuse myself. You want water? Wine? Beer? Soda?"

"Water, thanks. And you know more about what's good around here than me. Seven years, remember?"

Damned if he wasn't getting hard again from just watching her. "I'll use the other bathroom and leave this one for you. There are robes in the closet, if you're cold. Also, we still need to discuss the Ellie situation."

"Which reminds me... I'd better find my purse because I have a feeling I've got a few voice mails waiting."

"I'm pretty sure you left it in the elevator."

"Oh. Shit."

"Don't worry. It'll still be there." He stole another kiss, then went to take care of business. After a bathroom stop, he got a couple of bottles of water to take back to the bedroom. He didn't know about Sara, but he was chilly and couldn't wait to snuggle under the covers with her.

When he got to the bedroom, though, she'd turned on the lamp and she had her dress on. "You're not staying?"

"I would like to. Only, it's really late. And my mother's probably freaking out. I bet she's left two voice mails already. I don't want to not be there when they get up."

"I wonder if all mothers worry like that for the entirety of their kids' lives, or if it's just Italian mothers."

"I know for a fact that Italian mothers worry just as much long-distance as they do across the city. In college, God forbid I was two minutes late with our weekly calls."

He opened her bottle, and after handing it to her, he pulled on a pair of jeans and a T-shirt.

"Why are you getting dressed?"

"You think I'm going to just go to sleep while you head off by yourself?"

"You're worse than my mother," she said. "I know how to get home, Dom."

"Yeah? Remember how that turned out last time?"

She rolled her eyes. "I'm not going to walk from here. I'll catch a cab."

"And I'll accompany you until you're safely inside said cab. Or else you'll be getting more voice mails from me freaking out than you did from your mother."

Sara laughed. "You look kind of serious," she said, running her fingers over the light stubble on his jaw.

"I am serious."

"Wow, if you ever have kids you're going to be a real pain in their ass, aren't you?"

He thought about it for a second. "Probably," he said, cracking a smile and uncapping his own water. "You know I've lived here all my life, and I swear, it's like being on a separate planet from the rest of the world. You probably had a lot of adjusting to do in DC."

"That's true. But, you're a sophisticated man," she said, leaning over to bump his shoulder. "You know your way around more of Manhattan than most people from this whole community."

"I suppose so. And yet look what I found right here in my backyard."

Sara stooped down to look under the bed before he could see her face. "Do you see my sandals anywhere?"

He glanced around. "Could they be in the elevator, too?"

She straightened, blushing. "Here's the left one."

Dom wondered what that was about. He knew for a fact she hadn't found another woman's shoe under there. "Is there something weird under my bed?"

"What? No."

"Okay," he said, and scooped his slacks up from the floor. No sandal was hiding underneath. "So, Ellie."

Sara looked at him, a little smile on her lips along with a couple of worry lines on her forehead. "I've been thinking about what we said earlier, and well, you shouldn't pick me up tomorrow. You know, at my parents' place. It's better we meet somewhere."

"Because of Ellie?"

Sara sighed. "Yes. God knows I don't want to hurt her, even though I hate the thought of sneaking around. We're both too old for that and too busy, but really there are other good reasons."

"Such as?" He spotted her other sandal, half under his dresser.

"Our moms?"

Dom frowned.

"You don't think they'd call Father Michael and choose my bridesmaids the minute they found out about us?"

"Excellent point," he said, and picked up her shoe. "However, I'd have no problem telling them to chill. Nicely, of course. But firmly."

"Thanks," she said, as she sat on the bed to put on her sandals.

"What else?"

"Um, the neighborhood in general. The way Ellie's friends all drool over you, they'd probably boycott the pizza parlor in protest."

"Oh, for God's sake, they're just kids."

"Remember the teacher you had the hots for? Who was she, anyway?"

He shook his head, flashing back to sophomore year and the many times he'd gotten off picturing Mrs. Walker naked. "Don't even joke about Ellie and her friends anymore. Seriously."

Sara buckled the last strap and looked up, grinning. He caught her hands and pulled her to her feet. Her arms went around his neck and he held her tight. She lifted her lips for a kiss and he was happy to oblige.

He kept it brief, though. He was already semihard and tempted to strip off her dress. "What else?" he said, pulling back so he could meet her gaze.

"Oh, crap. I forgot. Tomorrow I work until eight and then I've scheduled an interview. Can we postpone things for a couple of days?"

He grinned at how concerned she looked. "Of course."

She blinked. "Anyway, not even counting the gossip-mongers, those are pretty heavy-duty reasons." He waited, as she stared back at him, worrying her lip. "I mean, I doubt we'll be able to hide things for very long. But, you know…" She shrugged and snuggled against him. When she turned her head and pressed her cheek against his chest, he knew that was the end of the conversation.

Putting aside his disappointment at delaying their date, Dom knew she was right. There were some very good reasons to keep things low-key between them.

But it was the one he was certain she'd left out that he was interested in.

13

SARA WAS SEATED across from Armanda Jacometti and her husband, Gaspare, in the living room of what used to be a notorious tenement in the heart of the old Little Italy. It had once been three apartments, but Paladino & Sons had remodeled the building, and made it a comfortable home for them and their four children, all of whom had moved out of the city.

The room itself was a tapestry of their family history, from the Victorian flocked wallpaper behind the plastic-covered couch that would have been at home in the 1930s, to the yellowed photographs in frames and on the walls. While there were some new things like a flat-screen TV and leather recliner, the overall feeling was of the past.

Sara had learned all of this before she'd asked her first question. But the wine was excellent, and Armanda Jacometti was turning out to be fascinating. A very good thing since Sara was having the worst time keeping her mind off Dom.

"Regina never really listened when Bisnonno, my great-grandfather, told his stories. She was too busy with boys. Obsessed with them. Day and night and day and night. But I listened. That's how I know what kind of life it was in the early days. He would tell us how, when he was a boy, they had no heat in winter, no air in summer. His parents worked all the time, and they barely could feed the family. He dropped out of school, which wasn't even a real school, when he was ten, and started selling papers on a street corner. Then he says nothing happened until he got married at seventeen, but I know a lot happened."

She glanced over at Mr. Jacometti, but his chin had hit his sizable chest and his eyes were at half-mast. So she probably wouldn't get to ask much about his family. Turning back to Armanda, she remembered something Regina had said. "I thought your great-grandfather worked for a newspaper."

"Worked? He made next to nothing. He had eight brothers and sisters, and they all lived in three rooms, and there wasn't even a toilet inside. But how he made some money that actually helped was doing work for *la Mano Nera*."

"The Black Hand. I read about them, but I thought they were only in Naples in the eighteenth century."

"They came here, too."

A movement caught Sara's eyes, but it was just Mr. Jacometti waking up a bit. Probably not for long.

"No one likes to talk about the Black Hand, let me tell you. You ask most of the people in church, and they'll say they never heard of it, but I know better. I found a letter once. Nonna caught me with it and burned it in the sink. Told me to forget what I'd read."

"Do you remember the letter?"

Armanda glanced at her husband, who hadn't said one word yet, but he was awake, eyes narrowed.

When Armanda looked at Sara again, it was with a sense of excitement. "It had a big picture on it. A knife dripping blood. It was from the leader of the gang, but he never said his name. Just that if Bisnonno, who was maybe twelve, thirteen, ever told anyone he was running for them, he would end up in a graveyard."

"Oh, my God. He must have been terrified."

"He never told us anything. I found that letter in an old book. Along with pictures of the family back in Italy, and my grandparents' wedding papers. That was only a year before he died, so I never asked him more about it. It was a scary letter, though. And once, when I was cleaning the altar at Blood of Christ, I heard that the children who worked for *la Mano Nera* earned more money doing dirty business than someone who owned a street cart. A good cart."

"That's amazing." Sara checked her recorder. It would kill her to lose any of this. "So, basically, they were gangsters?"

"They used blackmail. Not organized, not like the Mafia. Just bad men who got together and threatened good people who had next to nothing."

For a moment, she thought Mr. Jacometti was going to add to the story, but he just held up his hand. The gesture was one she recognized from her own father. It meant, "enough already" but Sara wasn't clear if he wanted his wife to stop talking altogether, or just stop talking about the Black Hand. She assumed it was the latter, judging by the subtle warning in his expression. It made Sara's blood pump faster.

Armanda shrugged. "I don't know so much about it. Just that people were scared, and people got hurt. Some even got killed. Did Regina tell you about any of that?"

No, she hadn't, so Sara running into Armanda at the feast had been very lucky. But she didn't want to press too hard and lose her source, so she changed the subject. For now. "She told me about the San Gennaro festival when Little Italy was still a big neighborhood. And about the cooking. My God, the recipes from your mother sounded so wonderful."

Armanda sighed. "When Mamma died, I did everything. All the arrangements. While Regina was at the house, taking all the recipe cards Mamma left for both of us. She tells me she's given me a copy of everything, but I know she keeps some to herself. Look what she brought to the feast, huh? That *pastiera* was Mamma's specialty."

Sara noted Mr. Jacometti's eyelids were drooping again. "Do you remember where your great-grandmother worked?" she asked Armanda.

"She was an *ostetrica*. A midwife. Busy all the time. She left her oldest daughter in charge at the house, but then Cherubina got a job at the Triangle shirtwaist factory."

"Oh, no."

Armanda shook her bowed head, then sipped her wine. She didn't have to explain that her great-aunt had died along with 145 other young women in the deadliest workplace disaster in twentieth-century New York.

Sara didn't want to leave on such a sad note, especially now that she needed to figure out a way to talk to Armanda again, without her husband. The woman knew more about the Black Hand, Sara was sure of it. "What was your favorite recipe that was handed down from your *bisnonna*?"

The pasta dish sounded great, but Sara's mind kept slipping back to this gang of extortionists. How had she known so little about this part of Little Italy's history? Now she had to make time to get to the library where she could start doing some real research. She had a feeling it would be well worth it.

Dom had wanted to know why she wasn't doing investigative journalism. With the fire that had been lit inside her tonight, her approach to the history of Little Italy was all about to change.

THANKFULLY, DOMINIC HAD finished going over the final checklist with the owners at the Chinatown renovation. Not that there'd been anything tricky in the job, but since he and Sara had hooked up, he'd found it difficult to keep his head in the game. Thoughts of her suddenly popped up at odd times. Quick images, sounds, even the memory of her taste. Once, right in the middle of a conversation.

But now he had a break before he had to meet Tony at the office. The walk would help him get back into his stride, in more ways than one.

When his cell rang, the number that popped up belonged to *New York Adventures* magazine. He grinned, figuring he'd made it to the next level of interviews, which was surprising, but good. "Dominic Paladino."

"Mr. Paladino? This is Brenda Oaks, Winona Donovan's assistant. She'd like to know if you're available to meet for drinks this afternoon at five-thirty."

For a moment, he just stood in the middle of the sidewalk as unruffled pedestrians brushed by. The request was completely unorthodox. Why the senior editor of *NYA* would be interested in speaking personally to someone who'd applied for the marketing and insights team made no sense, even if he had impressed HR. Hell, the magazine still managed to attract advertising rates high enough to keep the physical product—given away free in every corner of New York and New Jersey—more profitable than its very popular website.

Dom agreed, got the details and, as soon as he disconnected, called Tony to move up their meeting. Just so Dom would have time to run back to the apartment so he could change into a suit and also see what he could find online about Ms. Donovan.

By the time he'd made it to the bar at Betony on Fifty-seventh, it was as crowded with upscale drinkers as its

Michelin star deserved. A quick look at his watch showed he'd arrived for his meeting five minutes early.

Ms. Donovan, whom he'd researched as extensively as possible, had beaten him to the punch. She was at a small table, one slightly offset from their neighbor's, a champagne flute between her elegantly painted nails. She'd worn a silk blouse and a skirt and was sitting with her knees crossed perfectly, showing off her long legs and very high heels.

She was a beautiful woman in her early forties who exuded the kind of lifestyle the magazine was famous for. Young people, in age and at heart, living a cosmopolitan life in the most exciting city in the world. Her chic auburn hair was pushed back with a wide, pale band, her face had a healthy youthful glow, and her smile, when she saw him, withheld just enough to let him know she was in charge.

"Ms. Donovan," he said, holding out his hand. "It's a pleasure to meet you."

"And you, as well. Please, have a seat." She raised one hand, and by the time he was settled, a waiter was at his side holding an immense wine and beverage list.

"I'll have the Pilsner."

The young man bowed, and Dom was left with the woman who had been in the top twenty of *Fortune*'s Most Powerful Women three years in a row.

"A degree in finance," she said without preamble, "two masters' degrees, one in entrepreneurship and one in marketing and public relations, all with honors, and yet it took a rather long time to get there, wouldn't you say?"

"Yes, it did. I had to take some time off due to an illness in my family. As I'm sure you know, I work for Paladino & Sons, and I was needed there."

"Admirable. But wouldn't joining our team take you away from them?"

"They've known I wasn't going to stay in the construction business. While I'm good at my job, it's not my calling."

His drink arrived, and he took a sip, taking advantage of the break. He'd expected questions along these lines, but the way she studied him was intense. If it hadn't been a work meeting, he would have said it was predatory, as if she were scoping him out as a conquest. But he doubted very much that there was anything sexual happening. Unless she assumed that he'd be exactly the kind of man who would play up the sexual angle.

Tricky, but not unprecedented. That wasn't his game. And if it went on too long, he'd know the job wasn't going to work out for him. He just wished he understood why he was even a contender.

"I'm surprised you wanted to meet with me." He leaned in slightly. "I only had the one interview, with Alan Beckman."

"Which, as you know, was recorded. You handle yourself well, which impressed a number of my colleagues, as well as myself. Along with your video résumé, we watched several speeches you've delivered. The talk you gave at the BuildingsNY show last March was impressive."

"Thank you. Although it had very little to do with marketing."

She smiled, as if she'd been waiting for the comment.

"The reason I wanted to meet with you today isn't about the marketing position. I would like you to consider something else. Something new that we're spearheading here in New York."

He set aside his glass. "You've certainly got my attention."

She stared directly at him, hesitating just long enough to hammer home that she was in charge, and that she liked a slice of drama along with her champagne. "We're looking to hire a Director of Events."

The title was interesting. But vague. "And what's your vision for the post?"

"Instead of just listing major events in New York, we're going to start sponsoring some ourselves. We want to explore producing parties, screenings, concerts, but we want our events to be unique, which isn't going to be easy in this city. We want to make a big splash, attract a lot of attention straightaway. The Director of Events wouldn't be responsible for the productions themselves. You would be in charge of a creative team who would put together at least two major events per year. And you would be the public face of New York Adventures Productions."

The only thing about her pitch that excited him was the part where he'd work with a creative team. The part where he was "the face" sent all his red flags flying.

"Of course, more interviews would be necessary. You'll have to meet with publicity and marketing. And other key members of the team. This is a pilot program, remember, and even considering someone who isn't steeped in the *NYA* culture would be risky.

"However, it's very clear you're deeply invested in New York City. You have great appeal as a public speaker, and who knows? You might turn out to be just the breath of fresh air we're looking for."

"That's very flattering. Thank you."

Winona leaned in, her right elbow on the table. "If it goes as well as we project, our other branches will climb on board. Specifically, London, Los Angeles and Paris."

"All three markets that are already saturated."

"Exactly. What's already in place is becoming stale. People know about Lollapalooza and Burning Man and

U2 concerts. We want millennials and GenZ to come out in droves."

"It's a tall order."

"One I don't believe you'll have a problem with. Unless it doesn't appeal?"

"No, it's interesting."

"I'm sure you're curious about what a position like this would mean financially. That's not nailed down yet. I can say it will include excellent benefits, and we're considering a bonus structure, but even without those, we plan to be competitive. We're looking at close to six figures."

He honestly didn't care much about the money. It was more important for him to love what he did. Not that he'd tell her that. Even more appealing than the creative challenge, he was certain a job like this, done successfully, would open a lot of doors.

"You've given me a lot to think about," he said. "Give me a week. I'll let you know."

She looked surprised, but only for a moment. "A week will be fine," she said, then looked at her watch. "It's been a pleasure meeting you, Mr. Paladino."

He stood, waited for her to alight, and then offered his hand, which she took firmly before handing him her card. Then she was off, walking with the telltale grace of someone who understood her own power.

"OH, PLEASE." ELLIE spat the words, the look on her face one of furious betrayal. "You knew from the first day that I liked him, and you couldn't stand that he was nice to me. How could you be such a bitch?"

"It wasn't about you, Ellie. I'm sorry, but that's the truth. He was worried you'd be upset but I assured him you were too mature not to understand."

"Understand that you wanted him just to prove you're

better than everyone else? Or is it that you're trying to make Robert jealous?"

"Robert and I are finished."

Ellie's eyes narrowed. "Oh, yeah. Right. So that whole 'engaged to be engaged, then moving to Rome' thing was complete bullshit?"

Sara leaned against the door frame and wanted to cry. Ever since the morning after the feast, Ellie had been a terror. It was exponentially worse than Sara had expected. Even the other girls who worked at Moretti's were angry with her. And though Jeanette hadn't said anything, Sara had the feeling she was disappointed in her.

"Rome wasn't bullshit. But obviously I'm not going there now." Sara was ready to just shut herself in her bedroom until Ellie got her sense back. "Did you really believe Dom was going to ask you out someday? He's eleven years older than you."

The way her sister folded her arms over her chest and looked at her with such contempt made Sara feel sick.

"I knew it. I heard you had a crush on him in high school. That's why you broke up with Robert. So you could trap Dom."

"That's absurd."

"Oh, really? You must think I'm stupid. Every person at church has figured you out. Now everyone thinks my sister is a scheming slut. I hope you're proud of yourself." Ellie turned, flipping her hair over her shoulder, and marched off to her room as if she'd not just won the battle but the whole war.

Sara closed her door, then sagged against it. If this wasn't so heartbreaking it would be funny. Ellie was so young and soon enough she'd be over Dom and totally embarrassed by her crush. Just like Sara had been.

That humiliation wasn't something that would ever go

away for Sara, not now that she understood the depth of her foolishness. But she couldn't help thinking that maybe distancing herself from Dom would be for the best.

It would certainly ease things at home and work. And even though she had no regrets when it came to Robert, there might be a chance that Dom was simply a rebound fling. It all made complete sense. But she wouldn't be able to do it. Stay away from Dom. It was bad enough she thought about him so often.

After that incredible night and not seeing him for three days she missed him so much.

They'd spoken, twice, and she'd been the one to tell him maybe they needed to cool it for a few more days, until Ellie got over her jealousy. It was looking as if a few days wouldn't be nearly enough.

Anyway, all this madness had kept her too preoccupied to work, and that was crazy because she had that whole new string of inquiry to explore. If the Black Hand had been in Little Italy, why hadn't she heard about it sooner? It could just be some old tale that had stuck in Armanda's head.

Straightening up, she looked at her desk, then checked the time. If she got her act together quickly, she could spend at least an hour and a half looking through periodicals and newspapers.

Or she could call Dom and find out if he was busy tonight.

No. Not yet. The Black Hand search would require her full attention. She'd forget about Ellie, Robert, her parents. Dom.

Well, maybe not Dom.

Yes. Dom, too. A real reporter wouldn't let their personal life interfere with the story.

She put her laptop in her backpack, along with her tape

recorder and a notebook, and went to change out of her work clothes. When her phone rang, her heart seemed to skip a beat, hoping...

"Hey, beautiful," Dom said, before she even said hello. "What are you doing?"

"Why?"

"I have a surprise for you."

She'd barely shaken the image of her sister's angry face and here she was grinning like a loon, his voice stirring up butterflies in her stomach, among other things.

She really shouldn't.

"Oh, too soon?" His voice changed. "Are things not better with Ellie?"

"Not really."

"That's fine. It'll wait. You just tell me when."

She stared at her door, thought about how the night would go if she turned him down. "No. It's all right. We'll just meet somewhere."

"How about the corner of East Thirteenth and University Place. By the Union Square subway?"

"Okay. When?"

"How soon can you be there?"

"Twenty minutes. Unless I need to dress up."

"Nope. Wait. Have you had dinner?"

"No."

"Good. Oh, and Sara? I can't wait to see you."

The flutters got worse. Or better. She wasn't sure which.

14

Sara had ended up in a taxi, even though she should have taken the subway. Her hair hadn't cooperated, and then she'd smeared her eyeliner and had to start all over again. She'd worn one of her favorite dresses—navy blue with daisies on it that looked like spring—along with her navy ballet flats and tiny yellow cross-body bag, and it had only taken her five complete changes.

After leaving a somewhat cryptic note on the kitchen table, she'd left the house and spent her ride visualizing every worry and thought about her family floating away in an opaque bubble.

As soon as she stepped onto Thirteenth Street, she saw Dominic standing near the exit of the subway. Her breath left her on a sigh and she hoped his surprise was to take her right back to his place and do a moment-by-moment replay of the best sex she'd ever had.

It was evil, but fun to sneak up behind him and pinch his butt. Instead of jumping with a startled yelp, he just hummed low and sexy. "Finally," he said, as he turned around. "Oh. It's you."

Her mouth open, about to give him a what-for, she noticed he'd seen her coming up behind him in the big old ad window next to the subway entrance. "Spoilsport."

"I promise, the next time you pinch my ass, I'll jump like a frightened rabbit."

"Never mind that." She moved in closer at the same moment he did. Now they were just a handbreadth apart. "Why haven't you kissed me yet?"

"Good question." His hand skimmed under her hair until he'd cupped her nape, and then he pulled her into a kiss that quieted the whole of New York. At least, all she could hear was the pounding of her heart.

By the time they drew apart, his eyes were dark with wanting.

"Come on." He took her hand. "Let's get going. We've got a lot to do."

"Where?"

"Patience. I don't want to spoil the surprise."

After a few seconds of her scurrying to keep up, Dom slowed down to her pace. "I've been thinking," he said, keeping his voice just loud enough for her to hear over the city street. "Would it do any good for me to talk to Ellie?"

"And say what? That you were never going to go out with her, so suck it up?"

"I thought we might be able to come up with something a little nicer than that."

"I'm sorry," she said, sort of even meaning it. "I know you'd never be insensitive. But the situation has escalated way beyond reason. I honestly don't understand it. She has to know that nothing was ever going to happen between you two."

"I just hope I didn't do anything to encourage her." His thumb swept over the back of her hand, soothing her in all kinds of ways. "I used to tease her about the boys in school. I never considered it flirting."

"Of course not."

"I feel like an idiot not realizing she had a crush on me. It's just that she's so young. I like Ellie. She's always been a great kid, and I hate the idea of her being so upset."

"Me, too. Really. I do, and I appreciate you offering to step in. But can we not talk about it tonight? I need to give my brain a vacation."

"We don't have to talk about anything you don't want to," he said, then stopped just past the Basics Plus store, where there lived a bar with a black awning with white lettering. Bar 13.

Dom held open the door, and she entered a moody red-lit space with a tricked-out bar, a DJ playing loud music and an assortment of people dancing in a way that made them look cool.

Thankfully, since she'd never looked cool on a dance floor in her life, he led her to a staircase and past the second floor—where the hip-hop mixes weren't quite as loud—to a surprisingly quiet rooftop deck. This level was meant for talking, meeting, hooking up. Potted palms hid some of the less attractive neighboring buildings, and tall round tables, each with a big number thirteen drawn on the black base as well as the clean white top, didn't let people forget this was Bar 13. Dom swept her away to one of the very few empty regular-sized tables arranged around the perimeter. He held a chair for her before sitting himself, and that was when she saw the Reserved sign.

"You really had this planned out, didn't you?"

He grinned as a waitress came over holding two menus. One was for food, and the other—about three times the size—was their cocktail and wine list, opened to the Irish whiskey page.

"What is this?" Sara asked, taking the only menu that mattered.

"Part one of our own private whiskey walk," he said. "We missed the official one in March. We won't be going to all eight of the bars they recommended, but I know you have a fondness for the Irish stuff, so…"

"There are whiskey walks in the city now?"

"Every year."

"Wow. You remembered what I liked from the night when you got punched."

"I prefer to think of it as the night of our first kiss."

She couldn't believe it. In a million years, Robert wouldn't have done anything nearly as thoughtful. None of the men she'd gone out with would have. Yet another reason every woman who'd ever met Dom Paladino fell madly in love with him. He'd even remembered to make sure she wasn't working in the morning.

"I thought we'd get a couple of starters," he said. "And you can recommend the drinks."

Not that she was in love with him. Madly or otherwise. With the way he was looking at her, she had to rerun what he'd said before her thoughts had come to a grinding halt.

The starters. Right.

She cleared her throat and gave him a medium-watt smile. "Whatever you choose will be fine with me," she said, then she focused on the whiskeys. Some she'd tried before, others she'd never heard of. The name that popped was the Tullamore DEW. She'd never tried it but had heard good things, and it wouldn't break the bank.

Wisely, Dom asked for the hors d'oeuvres first, after making sure they wouldn't clash with their libation.

Once they were alone again, and she'd finally relinquished her menu, he put his hand over hers. "I'm glad you came out with me."

"Me, too." She almost admitted she'd missed him, but that would only send the wrong signal. "Even with Dad back, I've been incredibly busy. Getting good stuff for my thesis, though."

"Such as?"

"Have you ever heard of the Black Hand?"

"Is that a restaurant?"

"Then that would be a no. I interviewed Armanda Jacometti and her husband the other night, and she mentioned an extortion ring. They were around at the end of the nineteenth century up until about the 1930s. According to her they did some pretty nasty things. I haven't been able to find out much, only a few references on Wiki, but that's too unreliable a source for my needs. Guess I'll hit the public library and go through their old papers."

"You ask anyone else about it?"

"Not yet. And maybe it was my imagination but it sure seemed like it wasn't a subject Mr. Jacometti wanted to talk about. In fact, he gave Armanda a sign to shut it."

Dom grinned. "Which makes you all the more determined to dig."

"Well, of course, silly man."

"Now that sounds more like the reporter I used to know."

She stilled for a minute, remembering that "reporter" he used to know, and what trouble she'd caused Dom. But the sting wasn't so bad now that she'd apologized and he'd been gracious about it. She'd still like to punch that damn coach's lights out, but she and Dom were just fine. "You're right. I've missed it."

"What? Going for the jugular?"

Sara gasped, then tried to cover it up with a cough.

"No," Dom said. "That's not what I meant." He brought her hand to his lips and pressed a kiss to the back. "I like seeing the fire in your eyes, that's all."

"I know." She shrugged, still feeling the imprint of his warm lips on her skin. "I don't know why I reacted."

"Tell me more about the Black Hand."

She smiled. "I might be completely wrong, but it sounds like it could really be something. Armanda's sister didn't mention a word about blackmail or murder. Her tales were all about love and sacrifice and the kind of struggle where the good guys always prevailed. It'll be fascinating to find out which depiction is truer."

"Knowing what you told me about Five Points and Collect Pass Park, I'm betting on extortion."

She turned her hand until she could squeeze his. "I know, right? I'm really hoping it's true, because that will be the making of my thesis. Even I was bored with the nice, happy tales. I want both. Personal histories are like a giant game of telephone, told over decades. The more I can find about the facts and compare them to our parents' generation's idea of the truth is the heart of the project. And now, it's looking like it's going to be juicy as hell."

His laughter rose above the piped-in music, and it made her feel as if they'd truly taken a break from real life. The palm trees, this amazing whiskey walk, knowing that later she would be in his bed.

THANK GOD DOM had been going through several months' worth of *New York Adventures* magazines. He'd never heard of a whiskey walk until yesterday afternoon. The plan had come to him immediately, and even before he'd called Sara, he'd found out from Carlo that she wasn't scheduled to work that night.

He'd been to Bar 13 before for a private party held by one of his college friends. It had been easy to put the pieces together there, and at three other bars. It was entirely possible that Sara could have gone the whole eight, but he was a lightweight when it came to hard liquor. Now, a good red wine walk? That he could handle.

But this was turning out better than he'd even imagined. "I can ask my folks if they've heard anything about the Black Hand."

"Great. I really do hope there's something to the story. For all I know, it was just Mrs. Jacometti exaggerating to outdo her sister."

Dom laughed. "Yeah, what a neighborhood we live in, huh?" And yet he wasn't all fired up about trading it for Winona Donovan's world, though he should have been. "I'll mention it to my parents. I'm sure they'll tell you whatever they can. You speak Italian. Maybe Nonna remembers some things."

Sara's smile was brighter than the tall lamps dotting the rooftop. "Thank you. I didn't realize how unenthusiastic I was to do this research until I heard about this mysterious Black Hand. If it turns out to be nothing, I'll just move right into the gang wars. I know those were real and they weren't just Irish gangs."

The starters arrived, along with glasses of water, and shortly after came the whiskey. The waitress asked if they had any questions about Tullamore DEW, but since Sara had none, he didn't care.

She poured a tiny bit of water into her glass, swirled it around, then, with closed eyes, she took a sip. Dom watched her face, trying not to get distracted by the shape of her lips and how much he wanted to kiss her. When she smiled, he released his breath. "Good?"

"Very. I think you might like to add a little water to yours. Whiskey neat is something you have to grow into."

He took her advice, didn't close his eyes, had his sip, which burned on his tongue and down his throat. It wasn't terrible, but not something he'd order. He preferred icy cold vodka or mixed drinks that hid most of the alcohol taste. The pita and hummus they'd ordered would work. He dived in, right along with Sara.

"Tell me what's been going on with you," she said between bites. "We've barely spoken about anything but Ellie lately."

"I had an interesting interview."

"Oh?"

He didn't want to get into too much detail. Not this early in the process. He'd been doing a lot of thinking about the job on offer, and he kept getting stuck at being the "face." "*New York Adventures* magazine," he said. "They're looking to get into event productions, which would include being a sort of spokesman."

"Have you done that before?"

"Nope. But since I know marketing and promotion, I have certain talents they're interested in. It's all very preliminary."

"They're so well-known, though. We carry it on our magazine rack at the restaurant. They're showing up on every street corner. It might be exciting to work there."

"I don't know about exciting, but it may be a good way to make contacts for the future."

Sara put down her drink. "What kind of future?"

Dom hadn't been prepared for the question, although now it seemed an obvious one. In an attempt to draw out the moment, he took his second drink. Too much, it turned out, and while he coughed and Sara pressed her lips together so she wouldn't laugh, he stopped worrying about his answer.

After some water calmed down his esophagus, he dipped some pita, but didn't bring it to his mouth. "I'm interested in marketing, primarily," he said. "And promotion. But working from the inside. I've never wanted to be anywhere in the public eye."

Her eyes widened. "Are you kidding? I can't think of anyone more perfect. Plus you give great speeches."

"I know it doesn't make a lot of sense." He shrugged, not sorry he'd mentioned it, but the idea of discussing his reasons didn't appeal. "Wait. When have you seen me give a speech?"

"Let's not get sidetracked," she said, blushing. "Tell me what you meant. I'd like to understand."

He'd get it out of her later. "I'm not sure I can explain it, even to myself. I never had to work at it. Public speaking. It wasn't something I had to practice or learn. I memorized things, but that's not the same. It's like taking credit for having brown eyes."

Her head tilted, and just that little move made him want to forget about the rest of their tastings and steal her away to his place. "I can see that," she said, "but I don't know that I agree with it. It's not as if there's anything wrong with capitalizing on a natural gift. Imagine if Adele stopped singing because she was born having a great voice."

"I never claimed to be rational."

"No. You never did. But then, that's probably why I like you."

He grinned and slipped his hand over hers. "Not that I'm in any big rush," he said, "but we've got three more whiskeys to try before we can…"

"If you're trying to ask me if I want to go back to your apartment, the answer's yes."

He lifted his glass. "Then for God's sake, drink up," he said, even though he barely wet his lips with Tullamore DEW.

15

"WAIT." SHE PULLED back from the kiss just as the elevator doors were about to open. "Don't let me forget my purse."

"Got it." Dom tightened his arms around her and tried to get back to the business of kissing her senseless.

"Where?"

He sighed and lifted the yellow cross-body bag that was still attached to her.

"Oh," she said, giggling.

"Couldn't you feel it?"

"I thought it was—" she deliberately bit her lip "—something else."

"This tiny thing?"

Sara burst out laughing.

"It isn't funny," Dom said, leading her out of the elevator.

"I disagree."

"Why am I not surprised?"

"Hey." She tugged on his hand. "If it were the truth, then it wouldn't be funny."

"Okay, I can live with that." Dom stopped, lifted her purse from her and dropped it on the living room couch.

"And guess what?" she said. "Tonight was the best date I've ever had."

He put his arms around her and pulled her close. "But we haven't gotten to the best part yet."

Sara kissed him lightly, floating in a perfect buzz. She'd only had the equivalent of three drinks after she'd insisted they continue on. And the perfect amount of delicious food to balance things out. The whiskeys had been unique, each bar had offered an entirely different atmosphere and the kicker was that Dom had planned the whole thing just for her.

"I want to get naked." She ran her fingers lightly up the back of his neck as she teased his lips with the tip of her tongue. "I want you to get naked."

He started walking backward, never letting them get more than an inch apart. "I was going to grab us some water."

"No time," she said. "The situation has become critical."

"Really?" he said, looking terribly concerned.

She nodded, stumbling a little after stepping on his foot. "I can't even walk straight."

"Well, we have just had a lot of whiskey."

"Not that much. Anyway, it has nothing to do with booze," she whispered, her mouth close to his ear. Her whole body close enough, in fact, to feel his arousal pressing against her tummy.

Instead of the kiss she expected, he spun her as if they'd been dancing, held her around her middle and hustled them into his dark bedroom. After turning on the muted light of the wall sconces above the bed, he smoothed his fingers into her hair at her temples, his gaze fixed on her own. "Wow, did I not expect you."

"What do you mean?"

His fingers massaged her scalp in a way that made it impossible not to close her eyes. "I keep thinking about you."

"All good pure thoughts, I assume?"

"Not even close." He crushed her lips beneath his hot, wet mouth, his tongue hard and probing.

Sara trembled as he moved his hands over her back and cupped her buttocks, pulling her against his erection. A moment later, still holding her tight, he found the top of her zipper, and only struggled a second before he bared her back. Her lacy white bra was unfastened in the blink of an eye.

She tugged his shirt out of his pants, at least in the back, matching him move for move as he skimmed his fingertips down her spine before spreading his hands to rub as much of her as he could reach.

When she moaned, he stepped back, pulling her dress and bra down in one fluid motion, letting them pool at her feet. With a groan of his own, he cupped one of her bared breasts, squeezing gently, caressing the sensitive nipple that had beaded into a hard nub.

All the while, he kissed her, moaning as he probed and explored her mouth, their noses rubbing as he switched sides. She captured his lower lip between her teeth, pulling it gently before letting him go so he could take her mouth once more.

When her hand met with his belt and pants, she shifted so she could do something more than just touch now that they weren't sandwiched together. It didn't take much time to undo his belt, find and release the button on his pants and pull down his zipper. When she cupped his cock, so thick and firm beneath his silky boxer briefs, he groaned so deeply he lost the kiss, his forehead dropping to her right shoulder as he stilled.

"Take me to bed," she whispered as she attempted to divest him of his underwear.

Not quickly enough, evidently.

He took another step away, stripped his briefs down, pushed his shoes and socks off with his toes, then finally removed his shirt. When he looked back at her, it was as if he simply couldn't comprehend that she wasn't nude yet.

Laughing, she stripped, and he was so quick to lift her onto the bed, she still had one shoe on. Her lust-addled brain somehow noticed that the comforter and top sheet had been folded neatly at the foot. "So I'm a sure thing, am I?"

"Not at all," he said. "I'm just an eternal optimist." He rolled the two of them over so that she was lying on top of him.

"Is this a hint?"

His dark eyebrows came down for a second before he grinned. "Not intentionally. I want to do everything with you, although not necessarily all in one night."

"I think that would be quite ambitious."

"Ah, to be seventeen again," he said.

"Hmm, so you at seventeen meant—"

"Not talking about that.'

Sara laughed. It turned into a sigh as he touched her again, down and around, finally landing on her butt, which he kneaded, spreading her just enough to feel wicked. The motion also managed to move her against his cock.

"Sara, we have to stop," he said, doing just that.

"Problem?"

"Uh-uh." He leaned up, kissed her again, quickly this time, then rolled them both on their sides. Reaching over her, he had to really stretch, which trapped her face against his neck. She used the opportunity to breathe in deeply, welcoming the scent of him, something woodsy with a subtle hint of citrus. She loved that she had to get this close to really identify the scent. He should give lessons on how to apply cologne.

"Got it," he said. "Oh, sorry. Did I just strangle you?"

"It wasn't life threatening, so we're okay."

His smile was sweet, which didn't match the fire in his eyes. "Good. I have plans for you."

"Such as?"

"Be patient. It could be a…surprise."

Sara grinned when he kind of messed up the last word. "I'm beginning to suspect you can't hold your liquor at all."

"You're partly right. I'm a wine kind of guy."

"So, this evening was solely for me?"

"I managed to eke out a decent time."

Her laugh had him shaking his head. "I was pacing myself. Holding back for the main event."

"Oh," she said, arching her brows, all innocent. "You have some Jameson 18 in that fancy kitchen of yours?"

"God, you're sexy."

"Even when I'm teasing you?"

"Especially then. Now move. If we want to get this show on the road, I need to get this thing on."

"Let me help," she said, wrapping her hand around his aroused penis. She could feel the thrum of his heartbeat through the sensitive flesh when she gave him a light squeeze.

He choked on a laugh, then swore. "I ripped the condom. Happy now?"

"Shall I do the honors?"

He practically kneed her elbow in his haste to get another one from his nightstand. "Be my guest," he said, settling down next to her.

"Lie back." She pushed on his chest and didn't even look when he grunted as he landed, too caught up in opening the packet carefully.

When she had the round latex in her hand, she thought about putting it on him with her mouth, but the icky taste and the very unsexy possibility of choking were enough to scotch that plan. Instead, she gave the crown a lick that made him grunt.

"Whoa…" he said, grabbing a handful of her hair.

"Fine." Smiling, she tugged free and made sure when she used her fingers, she *really* used her fingers—rubbing a little, slipping underneath to touch his flesh, then squeezing his erection once the deed was done. She could actually feel him thicken in her hand.

Finally, she ran her hand down the inside of his thigh as she got to her knees. Since that made him close his eyes tightly, he hadn't noticed she was climbing on top of him, but he certainly did the moment she straddled him.

"Holy sh—"

"It was your idea. But if you want, I can move."

"No," he said, gripping her at her waist. "This is great. Really. Great. Perfect."

Bracing her palms on his chest, she raised up just enough to move into position. "Think you'll stay just like that?" she asked, bending low to check her target.

"I'm not taking any chances," he said, holding himself at the base.

She grinned, loving that he was so excited he'd gripped his lower lip with his teeth, and as she lowered herself down as slowly as she was able, his darkened eyes rolled up as his lids lowered.

Tempted to move more quickly, she forced herself to take it slow, although it was clear she should have worked harder on her quads, and not just relied on spin classes. But what was a little tension when she was making this gorgeous man moan as if he wasn't sure he would make it out alive?

When she hit bottom, he let out a huge breath. "Oh, my God…please move."

"What was that?"

His eyes flashed open. "I'm begging now. Seriously."

Instead of rising, she used her internal muscles to grip him as hard as she could.

It might have been too much.

The second she unclenched, he took hold of her waist

and lifted her straight up. Then, lowering her quickly, he stopped her progress halfway down until just the tip of his cock was inside her, before powering up again. Without his grip, she'd have fallen. It was the most erotic rodeo ever.

Waving one hand in the air wasn't the smart thing to do. He laughed and gripped her tighter, keeping them both in one piece.

"You're insane," he said, his next attempt at liftoff rather pitiful.

"I thought we'd established that a long time ago." Sara leaned down, moving her hips in a tight circle while she stole his grin.

Before she could catch her next breath, she was underneath him, his knees between her thighs, and he'd regained all the finesse he'd lost.

"One thing for sure," he said as he filled her until she gasped. "You drive me completely crazy."

Now it was her turn to meet his thrusts, and while she was no power driver, she was damned enthusiastic. And Dom…

He was just damned perfect.

DOM FIGURED THERE had to be another name for what they were doing. Because he felt *everything*.

She sighed and his heart beat faster. She thrust, and it was all he could do not to come on the spot. Her touch felt electric; her eyes drew him when any sane man would have looked away. It was as if they were plugged together, creating something brand-new.

He'd had enough experience to fully understand that this was not ordinary. Extraordinary didn't even cover it. He had no friggin' clue what was happening. All he knew was he didn't want it to stop. Desperate to go deeper, harder, he was helpless to hold himself back.

She opened her mouth, but instead of words, she made

a sound, her fingers digging into the back of his shoulders, the press of her legs urging him on.

Neither one of them closed their eyes. Until she cried out, nearly halting his hips with the strength of her orgasm.

Seeing her like this, her hair gone wild as she shook her head, her body trembling underneath him, blew him away. Each aftershock pushed him closer and closer to his own climax. Between one breath and the next, it was upon him. His muscles strained as if he were going to tear himself apart, his jaw so tight he could only groan, and he just kept coming.

It felt like a moment and an aeon until his body stopped straining. Until he could see again, look down into her astonished gaze. "So that wasn't just me?" he murmured, sounding as if he'd swallowed gravel.

She still wore the flush, from chest to cheeks. Even the tips of her ears were tinged pink. Gorgeous.

"Not just you," she whispered.

They stayed locked together for as long as he could, but finally his fatigued thighs had had enough. He was careful, leaving her. Both still trying to breathe normally, although he doubted they'd get there anytime soon.

He should have stopped for the water bottles. Parched as a desert, he tested his muscles, but nope, he wasn't going to make it all the way to the kitchen yet. In fact, he might end up staying just like this for the rest of the week.

"Yippee ki yay," she said, so quietly he might have missed it if it hadn't been between breaths.

Laughing actually hurt. Not that he could stop. When he was able to look at her, she was holding her chest with her arms crossed, giggling like a schoolgirl.

It was the best sound ever.

16

IT WAS A rare occasion that the whole Moretti family could sit down at the table together for dinner—one of them was usually at the pizzeria. Sara would be enjoying the experience even more if her sister wasn't still treating her like a traitor. At least Ellie saved the barbs for when they were alone.

Sara poured her parents and herself a little more Chianti since they weren't in a hurry to clear the dishes. "Pop, do you remember stories about your great-grandfather or what was happening around the time he came to Little Italy?"

Giorgio Moretti, known by all as Gio, nodded. "Some."

"I'm just starting to do some research on a group that sprang up in the 1890s. Did you ever hear anyone mention the Black Hand?"

He stared into his glass, nodded, took a sip.

"They were pretty horrifying. Threatening poor families with all kinds of nastiness, and I even heard they killed some people who didn't given in to their extortion."

Her dad looked at her mom for so long, Sara knew she'd hit a nerve. "Yes, my *bisnonno* knew about those sons of bitches," he said quietly.

In fact, everyone was quiet. Her dad didn't use that kind of language often.

Sara broke the silence. "Can you tell me what happened?"

"I only know what Nonno told me, and he didn't like to talk about it much. They lived in a tenement near here. It was destroyed by a fire a long time ago." He looked at Sara's mom again. "Rose, you remember when that was?"

She shook her head, her expression grim.

Shrugging, he continued, "They'd come over in 1894, and Bisnonno was a digger for the Public Works. His wife, my great-grandmother, who was also from Napoli, did piecework, as did the two older daughters. Their oldest son was a cripple, one leg shorter than the other, so he would be outside on Mulberry left to beg, while his little brother worked at a factory. I don't know what ages they were. Young. Very young."

Sara topped up her father's Chianti, and switched to drinking water. She wanted badly to go get her recorder, but she feared he would stop talking. Her father had never been big on reminiscing. Even her mother seemed surprised.

"He was a brilliant man, *Bisnonno*. After fourteen-hour days, he'd come home and work on his invention. A new kind of counting machine. I can't be sure, there are no papers left, but my father said it was going to be a big improvement on a machine called a comptograph, although he couldn't explain better than that."

"This isn't a good story," Rose said, picking up plates for the dishwasher.

"It could help me with my thesis, Mamma."

"The Black Hand found out that he was building something. When I say the Black Hand, it wasn't one big organization. It was little groups of thieves and bastards who didn't want to work like real men. They would copy the pictures from the newspapers. Skulls and bloody knives and nooses. There was no way to tell who they were because, by that time, everyone was a suspect or a victim, sometimes both. But *Bisnonno*, he had nothing to pay, and no one to explain that his machine wasn't even completely built. They barely lived hand to mouth, and they ended up eating spoiled food that the crippled boy would beg from the nearby pushcarts. It was no way to live.

"Then came the cholera, and the little girl died, and the threats, even with all the death around, got worse. They lived on the fourth floor. In one room. A fire swept through the building, and some said it was one of the lamps that tipped over, but everyone knew it was a lesson for those who didn't pay. The rest of the family lived in even worse conditions, but my great-grandfather's brother, his wife and two of his children died in the fire. Everything was gone, his machine, the piecework, all their savings, which were so meager it was barely enough to get through the next day."

Sara swallowed around the lump in her throat. Maybe it was because they were talking about her own ancestors she felt so awful. "They never found out who set the fire?"

"No."

"What happened to them?"

"They survived. Bisnonna worked at a factory, Bisnonno kept on at the Public Works, but they saw he was smart, and he ended up making a little more money. Enough. It was terrible, though. Nothing got much better for the family until 1930 when Mamma Moretti came over from the old country with her sauce recipe, and then everyone pooled together and started Moretti's Pizza."

"Our Moretti's?" Sara said, and she and Ellie looked at each other, for a few seconds, all animosity forgotten.

Gio nodded. "Somehow they got a deal on the building. And they saved enough to put in a big oven, and that was the start. People liked it. We still use the same recipe, almost. We updated a few things."

Sara was embarrassed that she hadn't known the origin of the restaurant, or thought to ask. "That was a terrible story, but at least it had a happy ending. I'm sure a lot of people didn't have that."

"The Black Hand was a scourge like cholera and dysentery," Rose said. "They only stopped when New York police got fingerprinting. It still took a long time to find any of those evil men. But by then, the Mafia had taken over the protection rackets."

"Not anymore, right?" Ellie said, her eyes wide.

Gio shook his head. "No. Not anymore. Anyway, it's time for my shows. I hope this thesis of yours isn't just about the terrible parts of our history."

"Not at all. Thank you for telling me, Pop." She got up and kissed his cheek. Then she helped her mother with the dishes, going over her father's story in her head, so she wouldn't forget anything. The moment she could break away, she would write it up.

She hadn't even noticed when Ellie had left the kitchen. Which was probably for the best.

TONY LOOKED AT his watch. Again.

Dom wasn't the only who noticed.

"Would you stop it?" Luca looked around the busy diner until his gaze rested on their waitress. "She's coming right now with the food. When's the last time the three of us sat down and had lunch together?"

"I'm as sentimental as you are, Luca. Wait, no I'm not, you little princess, but I told you I don't have a lot of time. I've got an appointment in an hour."

"An hour and fifteen minutes." Dom spread his knees,

enjoying having his side of the booth all to himself. It had paid to come early. It also felt great being at the Landmark Coffee Shop. The three of them had been going there for years, over the course of which most of their conversations had centered on sports and girls. "Besides, you can walk there in ten minutes, so stop being annoying and enjoy the moment."

Both his big brothers stared at him as if they were going to give him a lecture, but he just rolled his eyes and smiled as his cheeseburger and fries were set down in front of him.

"Anything else I can get you?" the waitress asked, smiling at Dom.

"No, thanks." When he looked back at the table, his brothers had already dug into their meals, the Philistines. But he was starving, too, so for the next few minutes the only sound was chewing. After the initial frenzy, Dom picked up his soda and studied it as if he'd never seen one before. "I got a job offer. Sort of."

"What do you mean, sort of?" Tony asked, at the same time Luca said, "Already? You've only been interviewing for a couple of weeks."

"It's with *New York Adventures*. And it's more of an offer to be considered for the position. There are still plenty of hoops I have to jump through."

"No kidding," Luca said. "We check out the events section all the time. Last month April dragged me to a hot sauce festival at the Brooklyn Expo Center."

Getting right to the point, Tony asked, "What's the position?"

"Director of Events. They're trying out a pilot program, sponsoring events instead of just providing information about them. They want someone to spearhead a creative team. Come up with ideas for new and different concerts or shows or whatever."

"Holy shit, Dom." Luca looked at Tony, then back. "That's fantastic."

Dom took anther bite of his burger.

"What are these hoops?"

He met Tony's eyes, and even though he knew his brothers supported him no matter what, he wasn't sure how much to tell them. "Mostly more interviews with whoever's in charge of publicity, marketing. Probably more that I don't know about yet."

"No sweat, right? You'll knock 'em dead, just like always."

Dom shrugged. "They also want me to be the face of New York Adventures Productions. If it works, then they'll start doing events in London, Paris and LA. If it doesn't…"

Tony stopped his fork halfway to his mouth. "They're not kidding around. That's a damn big opportunity."

"Maybe too big."

"Come on, you're not worried, are you?" Luca leaned back in the booth. "This was made for you. You'll kill it."

Shit. That was exactly what he thought they'd say. "Look, I'm just starting out. I've worked for our business all my life and I'm damn sure there's still a lot I don't know. A job this high profile my first time out? That's a pretty big tightrope to walk when I've never even been to the circus."

Tony elbowed Luca. "See right there. That's part of why they're interested in him. You've got a way with words, Dom. You always have."

Shaking his head, Dom snorted a laugh. Well, at least his brother hadn't said anything about his looks letting him skip a few rungs up the ladder. "I'm not even sure I want the job. I told her I'd get back to her."

"Who's her?" Luca said, although he was chewing his tuna melt, so it was hard to understand.

"The senior editor."

Tony frowned. "I'm not sure where the sudden cold feet are coming from, but if nothing else, you'll get to meet a hell of a lot of important people. Right?"

Dom nodded. "It's not really cold feet." He couldn't deny that Tony was right. Making connections was number one on his pro list. But the con list was pretty long.

"Well, what is it? What am I missing here? You've always welcomed a challenge."

"True. Still do."

"What I don't get is why you don't see this as an amazing opportunity." Luca's brows had gone down, and he'd pushed aside his plate, even though he hadn't finished his fries. "They clearly saw what we've known since you were a kid. You've been a charmer since birth, and I hate to admit it, but a lot of women think you're good-looking."

Dom made sure no one else saw him give Luca the finger.

"What?" Luca laughed. "I'm not saying it like it's a bad thing."

"Wait." Tony leaned in and lowered his voice. "Does it have anything to do with you and Sara? First you guys disappear from the feast last week. Then I heard you two were seeing each other."

Dom sighed. Not that he'd tell them, but the thought had crossed his mind. "No. It's got nothing to do with her."

"Kind of funny, though, huh? You dating Sara Moretti. I thought you'd sworn off local girls when you were eighteen."

"Don't you have somewhere else to be?"

Tony frowned and checked the time again, then gave Dom a dirty look. "Just because you're going to be the face of New York... We know where the bodies are buried, you little bastard."

Just hearing Tony mention that made Dom shut down inside. Talk about number one on the con side.

"Jesus," Tony said with a baffled look. "What just happened here?"

"What do you mean?"

"You should've seen your face."

Dom stuffed a fry in his mouth and just shook his head.

Luca joined in so now they were both staring at him as if he'd lost his mind. "Come on, bro. You know we're just yanking your chain."

"Yeah, well, everybody seems to think it's always a walk in the park for me. That I don't have to work at anything. Like I'm God's gift. Those people from *New York Adventures* don't know anything more about me than what they read on my résumé or observed in the span of a couple hours and they want to put me up front and center? And heading a creative team? What do they think? I'm gonna snap my fingers and come up with something no one's ever thought of before?"

Luca put down his sandwich. "I see your point," he said. "But we know you. And we know you can handle it. No denying it would be a hell of a challenge. But we also know how hard you've always worked. That you go at everything one hundred percent."

"Tell me this," Tony said. "Can you name one thing you've gone after that you'd really wanted and didn't get?"

"I don't think he's talking about girls," Luca added.

Dom laughed a little at that, then sighed and sank back against the booth. "I'm sure there are a number of things. I just can't come up with anything at the moment."

"I'm serious." Tony's brow furrowed, and his eyes were intense and probing. "No, I'm not talking about girls or free drinks or any of the shit you get because you're a good-looking guy. I mean the kind of thing that you've gone after, even though you had to work your ass off to get it."

Dom let his gaze wander out the window. "I know. You're right."

"Don't just give me lip service. You know how much that pisses me off," Tony said, sounding like such a grumpy old man that Dom had to smile. "Look, if you were good-looking and stupid? Man, that would be hard to take. But you're smart, Luca and I know it, the whole family knows. You're smart enough to go after what you want with everything you've got. *Capisci?*"

"Yeah, I know," he said, thinking how he should probably have eaten more than half his lunch. But his appetite had disappeared along with their teasing. Which wasn't like him. His brothers had always dished it out, and he gave it right back. "I still have interviews lined up with two other companies that sound interesting, and I've got some time on this. So anyway, Tony, you're really getting a bespoke suit from the in-laws? Whasamatta? Rentin' from Tuxes 'R' Us too good for yous?"

The tension left his chest as soon as the two of them laughed. He'd think about what his brothers had said. One thing he was clear on—he'd be foolish not to at least see what more *New York Adventures* had to offer. He'd call Winona Donovan tomorrow to ask about the next step.

17

DOM'S OLD MAN was waiting for him at the corner of Grand, right at the edge of the park that ran in a great broad swath across the Lower East Side. Kids were running all over the green grass, headed to and from the two big playgrounds.

Despite last year's scare, he looked nice and healthy. A little slimmer than a couple months ago, and he had color in his face. Retiring had been a good move, even if it had taken the whole family and both his doctors threatening him.

He noticed Dom approaching and smiled. "I used to come here to watch all three of you boys when you played ball here," Joe said when Dom reached him.

"I remember. This was a great place to hang out."

Joe looked up at Dom, who was several inches taller. "I liked what you said in your email about Collect Pond Park. Good, solid suggestions. We'll have to start with the attorney, see what's feasible."

Dom nodded. "You read that fast."

"I'm retired. What else do I have to do all day?" Joe put his hand in his pocket and rattled some coins. Just as he'd done as far back as Dom could remember. "And don't tell your mother what I just said. She'll make me paint the bedroom walls or something." He bent down to pick up a ball that had gotten away from some kids and tossed it to the boy running toward them. "Tony tells me you want to put some money into the church."

"I do."

"Even though the congregation gets smaller every year?"

"People still need that church, Pop. And a place for their kids to go that's safe. At dinner you mentioned a day care center. It's a good idea. After we build it, we could subsidize it so the people who can't afford to live in the city, but work here every day, have a place they can afford."

Joseph smiled. "You're a good boy, Dominic. Smart, too," he said, tapping his temple. "Always thinking ahead. You were right about making the trust more relevant. I was busy with the business and didn't give it serious thought. But now…" He turned back to watch the kids playing ball on the grass and shrugged. "Now your mother is driving me crazy. I can't say anything about the trust or pick up a hammer without her accusing me of ignoring the doctor's orders."

"She means well, Pop. Anyway, she knows we're working together on the changes. She hasn't told me to keep you out of it."

"I know. She still drives me crazy. Wait till you're married forty years, you'll understand." Joe smiled and clapped for a kid who'd just hit a ball over to the next borough. "I have to ask you something. About the trust. Tony's got his hands full with the wedding and the business. Luca's crazy in love with his girl and his carpentry. What about you talking to the lawyer and the accountants? Figure out what we should do next?"

Surprised, Dom studied his father. "Why don't you do it? I doubt Mom would mind. It wouldn't be stressful."

"What's the matter? You don't have time?"

"It's not that… Have you mentioned this to Tony?"

"Why? You know what you're doing. I have complete faith you'll handle it well. And before you say that you might get a job that will keep you too busy, I know that. And if it happens, we'll work it out. But for now, I would appreciate it if you could make a few calls. Find out what we can do, what the limitations are with the public property and with the church, and the school, too. Call Father Michael and Archbishop Thomas. And also, talk to the mayor and the county commissioner. See if we can't fix some of the roads out here. Huh? What do you say?"

Dom had expected the conversation to be about his new ideas for the money held in trust, but what his father was asking was a lot more than that. Even though he was moving forward with *NYA*, he hadn't been offered the job, nor did he know if he'd accept it. And he hadn't been so interested in anyone in a long time, but now, at the worst time possible, he wanted to see a lot more of Sara.

But this was his family legacy, and they weren't talking about just a few million dollars. The trust was well padded. It could make profound changes in the community. And his father wouldn't ask if he didn't think Dom could do the job. "Sure, Pop. I'll start making calls tomorrow."

"Some miracle, huh?" Joe said, continuing to watch the kids. "All these years, five generations of Paladinos and no one outside the family ever knew about the trust. No questions. No suspicion."

"Everyone was afraid to ask questions. They were worried their rents would be raised."

Joe laughed. "True."

"You deserve a lot of credit, Pop. The funds tripled while you were in charge of the trust. After we get squared away in this new direction, we won't have to keep everything a big secret and I—"

"Wait, wait." Alarm darkened his dad's face. "No one can know the Paladinos have been subsidizing rents all these years."

"No, of course not. I meant whatever we do in the future, in the parks, for instance… I don't see why we can't have a small plaque on a bench or on a fountain with your name on it. Let people know you're helping the community."

Joe smiled. "You boys, your mother and I are so proud of the three of you. Worth so much money you don't have to work a minute in your life and yet you all work harder than anyone I know. No one has taken money from the trust for themselves—that's why it's well funded. If we have any plaques they're going to say the Paladino Family."

Dom nodded, letting a breath out around the lump in his throat. He knew better than to argue about something like this. Joe Paladino would never take credit for anything. Dom owed his great work ethic to his old man. Both his parents. He doubted it had ever occurred to Tony or Luca, just as it hadn't crossed Dom's mind to touch the trust for personal gain. They were all grateful to have been given the privilege of choosing their own home in the community.

They walked in relative silence the short block from Forsyth Street to Chrystie, where Joe was going to meet some friends for coffee. He held out his hand, and after Dom shook it, he pulled his dad in for a big hug.

"You'll do us proud, son. And don't tell your mother I was behind this."

Dom smiled. Damn, it wasn't going to be easy to leave the family business.

AFTER DOM LEFT his dad, he headed toward Mulberry, trying to figure out how he was going to work, go on interviews, cover for Tony until after his honeymoon and take on more of the trust. When he reached his folks' house, instead of hitting his mom up for a lunch of leftovers he knew he'd find, Dom walked three more blocks.

He couldn't see Sara inside Moretti's, but she was probably in the back. He knew she was working today, and while he hadn't planned on stopping by, he really wanted to see her.

Jeanette was behind the counter, and Djamila, one of Ellie's friends who'd been working there for a while, was serving a large pizza to a group of middle-aged men. The lunch rush was over so the place wasn't very crowded.

He walked up to the counter just as Ellie came out from the back.

Her step faltered when she saw him, but she regained her poise quickly, offering him a smile that looked genuine as she went past him to serve a couple of slices to a kid sitting near the window.

"Hey, Dom," Jeanette said. "I'm just about to take my break, but if you want me to get your order in real quick, I can."

"That's okay. I'm in no rush."

Ellie replaced her at the counter, her long hair done up in an elaborate twist with tufts of hair sticking out in a couple places. "What can I get for you?"

Knowing what he did now, he easily noticed the flirty way she tilted her head. "How about a couple of combo slices?"

"Sure," she said, quickly slipping his ticket on the order wheel. "If you wanted to see Sara, she had to go to the market. Genius didn't order enough mushrooms."

There it was. The snark he'd expected. Worse, actually. That tone of Ellie's reminded him too much of the mean girls he'd known at that age.

Instead of coming back to the counter, she stopped at the soda fountain and poured a soda he figured was for him. It was.

"What? No one ever makes mistakes here?" He said it teasingly, but he saw that Ellie got the message.

Her cheeks splotched a little pink. "Yeah, well, Queen Sara never gets anything wrong, don't you know that? She knows more than anyone about running the restaurant. Guess she majored in journalism and pizza at college."

Another girl, her name escaping Dom at the moment, came out from the back, tying her apron on. She smiled at him in a way that didn't fit well any longer, but he was much more concerned with the obvious grief Ellie was handing out not just to Sara, but about Sara.

He put on a nice smile and kept his expression friendly. "Ellie, would you mind if I talked to you for a minute? By the magazine kiosk?"

She shrugged as if it was no big deal, although she stood up a lot straighter, then turned to the new girl. "I'll be right back," she said. "Table three is waiting on a pepperoni."

Dom knew what he was doing was risky. He needed to be careful not to make things worse between the sisters, but he couldn't just let this shit pass.

"What's up?" she said, standing with her back to the corner and facing him.

"I couldn't help noticing the friction between you and Sara lately."

"Why? What did she tell you?"

"Not much. That's why I'm asking you." He didn't seem to be making headway. The defiance in her eyes showed him another side to Ellie—it reminded him that, in many ways, she really was still a child. "Normally I wouldn't stick my nose in this, but I can't help thinking this is somehow my fault."

Ellie looked more wary now. "Well, it's not," she mumbled, the words barely audible.

"It seems the problem started the night she was almost assaulted and ended up patching me up, so what am I supposed to think?"

"It's her," she said, looking away. "Not you."

"Okay, look." Dom took a breath. "You know we went to Loyola together. She was a year behind me, but I knew who she was. But not for the same reason I'm sure all the guys know who you are. Sara wasn't pretty back then. She was skinny and wore glasses, had braces. She hid behind her long hair and sometimes wore this really awful hat. Guys used to make fun of her. Behind her back mostly, but I'm pretty sure she knew."

"Sara? Ugly? I doubt it."

"Go check out her yearbooks if you don't believe me."

"Okay." Ellie's whole body was on the defensive. She folded her arms across her chest and was looking at him as if she'd already made up her mind not to believe a word he said. "Fine. Sara used to be ugly. Boo hoo. Well, she isn't anymore, as you've noticed. And she thinks she can do anything she wants."

The last couple of words wavered, and for a minute, Dom thought Ellie was about to cry, but he had that all wrong.

"Has she mentioned Robert?" Her voice had risen. "The guy she lived with at college?"

Robert? He sure as hell would have remembered. But then, that was before. She had no obligation to tell him a thing about what she did at GWU, just as he wasn't about to tell her about his private life. "No, she hasn't."

"Then I guess she forgot to mention she's supposed to meet him in Rome when she's done with her thesis." Her defiance had turned to a look of victory. "That should tell you a lot. And in case she conveniently forgets, what with her being the queen of Little Italy now, you should know they're engaged to be engaged."

Her words felt like a blow to the gut.

He tried to keep his expression neutral, careful not let himself get caught up in the drama. Ellie was seventeen, a horrible age for hormones, and he supposed she felt embarrassed that she'd had a crush on him when he was so obviously into her sister. She could be making this all up.

It didn't matter. He wasn't about to let this normally sweet girl twist things around in an attempt to make him change his mind. Ellie needed some facts. "Let's just get back to what I was saying, all right? And please, try to listen with an open mind. As a favor to me?"

The anger seemed to go down a few notches, at least what he could see on the outside, and he jumped right in.

"When Sara was thirteen and I was fourteen, I did something pretty damn unforgivable to her. Something I'll always regret. My mom tried to make me ask her to the spring dance. I was talking to some of my buddies about how I would never go with her, no matter what my mother said. Because—" Dom was sure repeating the words out loud would kill him. He'd drop right on the spot. Reminding himself he'd been a kid and kids often said thoughtless, cruel things did nothing to ease his self-disgust. "Because she was ugly. And flat-chested. And weird. And I'm pretty sure I called her a nerd." He inhaled another breath while he still could. "Remember, I was a popular guy. Had my pick of the juniors and seniors. The point is, Sara was around the corner and heard me. Every horrible word."

Ellie blinked and bit her lower lip just like her sister did, although the concern didn't stick.

"It didn't help that she was painfully shy back then."

"Sara? Shy?"

"Crazy shy. And me and my big conceited mouth must have crippled her."

Ellie shook her head. "There's no way you did that. You're like the nicest—"

"I'm not lying. You think it's easy for me to admit I was that much of an asshole? If I was going to lie, I'd try to make myself look better than that."

"Yeah, but you could still exaggerate so I'd feel all sorry for her."

"Come on, Ellie, this isn't grade school." He sighed when she flinched. "Anyway, I don't need to exaggerate. Pull out her yearbook. And once you've taken a good look, try to imagine what your life would be like if you hadn't turned out so pretty."

Her blush was quick, and it made her duck her head.

"You know exactly what I'm talking about. You were a beautiful child and now you're turning into a beautiful young woman. You're confident and outgoing. The only place Sara had ever been remotely like that was when she'd worked on the school paper, and because I'd been so cruel, she later retaliated by writing the article that got her kicked off the paper for the rest of the time she was at Loyola."

"Well, that was stupid. She shouldn't have done that."

"You're absolutely right. She had no business writing something she knew was false. I'm not defending what she did." He'd kept the girl longer than he'd intended. But no customers had come in, or at least he hadn't heard the bell over the door, so Ellie was just going to have to hear a little more. "That said, I don't believe she should have been taken off the paper as punishment. Sara made a mistake…we all do. But you and I both know how being one of the popular kids lets you catch a lot of breaks. She caught none."

Ellie wasn't exactly repentant, but neither did she look as defiant as she had before.

"I know you've realized that I'm interested in Sara. I have no idea why but, luckily for me, she decided to give me a second chance I don't even deserve. It's been a long time coming."

The way Ellie stared at him—through him—made it clear she was thinking of someone else.

"One last thing. And I mean it. I'm not interested in Sara because she's pretty. It doesn't hurt, I'm not going to lie, but there's so much more to her. I want to know Sara because she's a remarkable person."

Ellie took in a deep breath and actually met his eyes. "Okay. But that doesn't make it all right for her to act like she knows everything about everything."

Dom held back a laugh. "Well, I'll leave that part for you two to work out."

She almost smiled.

"Okay, I've kept you long enough—"

The door opened, and Sara, carrying a shopping bag stopped, worry spreading across her face at seeing the two of them huddled together.

Ellie took a step, hesitated, then offered Sara a tiny smile, before hurrying to cash someone out.

"What was all that about?" Sara asked, meeting him halfway.

"I think my pizza's getting cold," he said, taking the bag from her, then giving it up to Jeanette waiting at the counter.

"Dom…"

"It was a private conversation between Ellie and me," he said, noting the girl's little grin. "Nothing to worry about. I promise."

Sara sighed, skewering him with a suspicious glare.

Dom just smiled. "I was wondering," he said, loud enough that everyone near the counter and behind it could hear, "if you'd like to have dinner with me tomorrow night."

She stared at him as if he'd lost his mind.

He looked at Ellie, Djamila, Jeannette and the blonde who was holding two slices of pepperoni. "Anyone have a problem with that?"

18

SARA SLIPPED HER flash drive into the Forty-second Street library's computer to download another article she'd found on the Black Hand. It was from the New York Tribune, dated 1889, and it was more of an obituary than an article; the death of an elderly Italian man, patriarch of a large family who'd come over from Naples. He'd been beaten by an unknown gang on Hester Street, and the police had found part of a note that had the signature drawing of a black hand holding a dagger on the header. She downloaded the sepia-toned wrinkled picture, although she was more interested in the name of the deceased. Olivet. Just like the Olivet family who'd lived down the street from Sara's family.

She made a note to get in touch with Gabby Olivet, who'd been her mother's friend since childhood, then panicked when she noticed the time. Dom would be calling soon, but there was still so much to research. Of course, she'd be coming back. Since her focus had shifted to the Black Hand, her thesis was taking an interesting twist and she needed to do a lot more than chronicle the immigrant families' stories. It was critical to record as many histories as possible.

At the same time, she needed to gather reliable data from the earliest immigrants. She'd had no idea the depth of the reportage that survived in the digitized articles from the *Tribune*, the *New York Times* and the *Wall Street Journal*, all dating back to the early to mid nineteenth century.

She went back to the computer, and found a police report that had a long list of names, all supposedly linked to the extortion rings.

The sound of her phone made her scramble to answer it before she got herself kicked out.

"Hey, gorgeous."

Dom's voice made her smile. "Hey."

"I gather you're still at the library. Or else you're whispering because you want to have phone sex."

She laughed, covering her mouth. Actually phone sex in a library sounded kind of exciting. Risky, though. She didn't need to be barred from the best resource she'd found. "Yes, I'm at the library."

"Damn. Maybe another time. How's it going?"

"Better than I'd imagined. There's so much material from the mid-1800s on, from so many different sources. Thank goodness I brought my 128-gig flash drive."

"There's that much?"

"Probably not. Listen to this. Three tenements were set on fire within a span of one week in 1887. No one died, but some kids were hurt, and seven families were displaced. The fires were traced to three different gangs, all claiming to be the Black Hand. Most of them weren't gangs at all, just a few desperate men who'd heard about the racket and were trying to cash in. It's actually sad and tragic."

"You're sympathizing with the extortionists?"

"No. Yes, kind of. What wouldn't you do for your family? I'd like to think I wouldn't steal or hurt anyone, but I've never been in such dire circumstances."

"Huh. That's actually a lot to think about. I wonder if there are any accounts from the blackmailers in those archives. It would add a great slant to your thesis."

"I know. The more I learn, the more excited I get."

"Okay, now I really want to see you."

Sara grinned. "You trying to weasel out of buying me dinner?"

"Nope. Too many witnesses yesterday. How about Chinese? I was thinking—"

She lost what he was saying when she got to the next line. In a list of names one stood out: *Valente Paladino*. The sentence after that was just as shocking. *Considered a ringleader on Mulberry Street*.

"Hello?" Dom asked. "You still there?"

"Yeah. Yeah, sorry. Something in this article caught my eye."

"You think you'll be done soon?"

"Uh-huh," she said, scribbling the names as fast as she could, even though she would download the whole page after she'd closed it.

"Good, because I'm…" His voice changed. It was no longer coming from the phone but from behind her. "Already here."

She nearly jumped out of her skin, her finger instantly hitting the page down button several times. "You scared me."

He leaned over and kissed her. "I didn't mean to do that. Sorry."

"No, it's okay," she said. "It'll just take me a minute to wrap things up. Where were you thinking about eating?"

He walked around the table and pulled out a chair.

"I'll only be a minute," she said, ignoring the temptation to just stare at him.

Wearing a white shirt, with the sleeves rolled up to his

elbows, his tie askew, his top button undone, he looked sexy. Her heart had already been beating fast because of what she'd seen on the screen, but now…

With the reminder of what she saw, she got a bit manic in her rush to put her notebooks away, unplug her flash drive and zip up her backpack. There was no need to jot down her place in the *Times*—she'd never forget it now.

Dom pushed the chair back in as she turned off the machine. "That's it?"

"That's it," she said, hoping that the name in the paper meant nothing.

Dom came around the table, slipped her backpack over his shoulder, then stole a kiss that wasn't meant for a research library.

Everything else that had busied her mind for the past several hours drifted away on his taste, his scent and the way he used his mouth to show her what he wanted for dessert.

When they finally pulled apart, he looked deeply into her eyes. And there was that frisson thing again. Only this time it didn't just travel down her back, but all the way to her toes.

She forced herself to step back before they did something they'd regret. "Did I tell you I got two calls today? People wanting me to interview them. Both women said they know about the Black Hand."

"At least the gossip chain is working in your favor."

"Yeah, I hope it keeps on going."

As they approached the exit, Dom slipped his arm around her shoulders. "So, Robert?"

She stopped dead. "What?"

"Ellie mentioned him yesterday. I know it's probably none of my business and if you don't want to talk about it, that's fine."

"No, I don't mind," Sara said, and she really didn't, but she had to wonder what Ellie had told him. "Robert and I were together for two years at GWU, both majoring in journalism. He left for Rome to make some connections in the Vatican a couple of months before I came home. The plan had been for me to finish my thesis, then join him there. It didn't take long for that to fall apart."

"I figured it had to be something like that."

"I wasn't hiding anything."

"Oh, no. It wasn't an accusation." Dom tightened his arm around her as they reached the exit and walked down the steps between the two lions. "Ellie was still mad at you when she told me."

"It's getting better between us," she said. "It's fine that neither one of you will tell me exactly what happened. Sort of. We're not exactly besties, but the verbal jabs have stopped."

"Good. And if you really want me to tell all, I will."

"No. It's okay, but I reserve the right to change my mind."

He walked them to the curb and stuck out his hand. The traffic was crazy, so it wouldn't be a quick ride to Chinatown. "You think you guys broke up because of the long-distance thing?"

She sucked in a breath.

"Hey, sorry, I shouldn't be asking."

She shook her head. "The reason I hesitated was that I'm kind of embarrassed to tell you the truth."

"So don't tell me." Dom smiled. "It's okay."

Sara thought for a moment. "I let him manipulate me," she said. "I just didn't realize it until a couple of weeks ago—"

"Sara, honestly, I—"

"I want to." Snuggled up against Dom's hard body, she

felt brave. And happy. She'd never felt this way with Robert. "We were both focused on investigative journalism. But I always got better grades, more articles in the school paper. Oh, and we first met in Italian class, of all places. I was already close to being fluent, and he'd always had a thing about the Vatican. A year ago he started pushing me toward human interest stories. Trying to convince me that was where my real talent was. I feel foolish that it took me so long to realize he didn't want the competition."

Dom lowered his arm, even though no cab had stopped. He studied her, his face solemn. "That complaint to the school board and then the fallout probably had a lot to do with your willingness to believe him. You were young. I can see how something that traumatic could make a person vulnerable to manipulation."

It was Sara's turn to search his eyes. "I hope you're not thinking any part of what happened to me was your fault. I made a very bad choice. But I think you're right. It did make me doubt myself."

"I'd still like to punch out Coach Randal."

"Well, then I'll hold him down for you."

"That wouldn't be necessary."

"Show-off," she said, squeezing his hard biceps.

Dom smiled and pulled her close. "You're a strong woman, Sara, and your ethics and values are going to make you a great journalist. Don't let anyone tell you otherwise."

Sara's eyes misted and she buried her face against his shoulder. She doubted he'd ever know just how much his support meant to her.

"COME IN, COME IN."

Mrs. Di Stefano led Sara into her beautiful Queens town house, with elegant drapes, a Persian rug framed by a gleaming hardwood floor and a portrait of what Sara guessed was a matriarch from the old country above the fireplace.

"Thank you for seeing me," Sara said, and sat on the couch across from a pair of wing chairs. "You have a lovely home."

The older woman, who was as polished as her surroundings, beamed. "Would you like some sangria?" She gestured to the pitcher sitting on the coffee table between them. "It's an old recipe from my mother, but if you'd prefer I have sparkling water and tea."

"I'm fine for now. Although I'd love to try some sangria before I go."

"Yes, of course." She sat in the wing chair and watched as Sara brought out her recorder and notebook. "This research about *la Mano Nera* is for school?"

"My master's thesis, yes. As I mentioned, I'll be recording our conversation, all right?"

Mrs. Di Stefano nodded, and with pen in hand, Sara turned on the recorder.

"I heard many stories about the Black Hand, mostly from my husband's grandmother, who lived with us for many years before she passed. She wasn't a morbid woman, in fact, she used to talk more about her mother's stories of elaborate puppet shows, and how before La Guardia became mayor, there were organ grinders throughout the city, with their dressed-up monkeys, collecting pennies and nickels in tin cups.

"But she also remembered some terrible things. Her uncle worked at Penn Station, which was a very good job at the time. He'd learned to speak English, so he sold tickets for the steam trains." Mrs. Di Stefano stopped. "I have cookies. Would you like some?"

"No, thank you." Sara smiled graciously, but all she wanted was for the woman to keep talking.

"He brought home more money than a lot of other men living in the old Little Italy. Now it's East Harlem, but back then, it was all Italian. He received a letter with a handprint, big, black ink, in the center of the paper, with a drawing of a dagger. It wasn't that unusual, and he knew that if he didn't pay what they wanted, they could hurt his family.

"The story went that he paid a large sum to the blackmailers. Maybe the equivalent of three thousand dollars. Much more than was typical. Usually, they asked for a hundred, maybe two. So, he paid the money, and it was very hard for a long time. At least he was alive. His friend, who also worked at Penn Station, was strangled and his body burned after he refused to pay."

"Oh, God."

"Everyone knew. They wanted to create fear. People became suspicious of neighbors, of relatives. It wasn't an easy life in those days."

"Your husband's grandmother, did she mention her uncle's name?"

"Orsini. Jacopo Orsini."

Sara recognized the name. He was one of the men listed in the police report, although not as a victim. "That's fascinating," Sara said, pulling out one of the documents she'd copied at the library. It was easy enough to find Orsini's name on the list. "I found a reference to a man by that name, on a police report from 1903. He was arrested for extortion and threatening a family with violence."

Mrs. Di Stefano looked utterly horrified. "That's someone else. There must have been a lot of people with that name. It wasn't her uncle."

Sara had done a more detailed search on the names from that report. "It says here that he was married to Elena Passerini and had brothers named Taddeo and Isidoro."

"Impossible." She stood up, looking at Sara as if she'd been responsible for the arrest.

"This information is from the public records. I can show you, if you like."

"Those records are lies. I think it's best if you leave now."

Sara was stunned into stillness. This morning she'd been worried that she'd have so many stories that there would be arguments and contradictions. It never occurred to her that anyone would actually be upset by something that had happened generations ago.

"My wife would like you to leave."

Sara jumped at the deep voice. Mr. Di Stefano had come from the hallway.

"I'm sorry, I don't understand. This isn't a reflection on you. Anyone researching the Black Hand would see these records."

The man's hands, Sara noticed, had fisted. There was clearly no use arguing with either of them. She quickly gathered her things, glad she'd gotten their reactions on tape, and was shown the door.

"You have no right stirring up trouble," Mr. Di Stefano said tightly and slammed the door. But his voice carried through, loud and angry. "I told you not to talk about the past. Now look what you've—"

Sara turned around to stare at the door, which had nearly smacked her in the ass. What the hell had just happened? She'd been so excited about this interview. Did Mrs. Di Stefano honestly not realize her husband's relative had become part of a Black Hand gang? Or had she hoped that Sara would print her revisionist history and change the past?

Walking slowly toward the subway, Sara felt more dejected with each step. By the time her train came, she wasn't even surprised when she got a call canceling her three-thirty interview. No reason was given. Just a flat refusal. Only fifteen minutes since Mr. Di Stefano had kicked her out.

If it was this bad with strangers, how on earth were the Paladinos going to react when she brought up Valente? She'd discovered much more than that one allegation. Ultimately, he'd been convicted of extortion. She hadn't even mentioned it to Dom. But tomorrow she was supposed to go with him to the Paladinos' for dinner.

By the time Sara got home it was almost one, and she was still shaken. A fresh change of clothes and putting her hair up into a boho updo lifted her spirits. In fact, she'd decided that just because a couple of people had overreacted to the truth, that didn't mean anyone else was going to.

Her next interview would be better. Thankfully, it was much closer. Five blocks from her folks' house, although she didn't know the family well. Lily Finoccio and her husband weren't big churchgoers, just showing up on the holidays. Their children were several years older than Sara and no longer lived in the area.

When Sara knocked on the door, Lily opened it quickly, although not by much. "I'm sorry, Sara. My husband isn't feeling well. We'll have to cancel today."

It was hard to keep her smile in place, especially because she'd seen Al Finoccio at the corner bodega on her way out to Queens earlier. He'd certainly looked fine chowing down on an apple fritter and coffee. "I hope he feels better soon."

Lily gave her a half smile and closed the door.

Strike three. Or was that four?

She had only one more appointment today, an older widow who might not have heard that Sara was a pariah yet. How was this horror spreading so fast? It was insane.

Since she had some time, she decided it would be harder to turn her away if she came bearing pastries. So she hopped on a bus to the bakery and used the ride to try and wrap her head around what was going on.

What shocked her most was even though Little Italy was a shadow of its former self, there was still this unnerving rumor mill. Back in high school she'd actually written a short paper about it, comparing the outbreaks to wildfires. Easy to start with a casually tossed word, quick to spread, but also, fast to douse—as long as there was another fire in the wind.

She entered the bakery, one of the most popular in the area, so no surprise there was a line. While she waited, Sara let her mind go to the one place that had kept her sane today—thoughts of Dom. He was working on Broome Street, where Paladino & Sons were going to transform a condemned building into a boutique hotel.

At least she'd see him tomorrow night—

She thought she heard her name.

Itching to silence the chatting women behind her, she could do nothing but wait and listen, even as she told herself she was being paranoid.

"She comes back to town, telling lies, that Sara Moretti. Jane Landi told me that Sara made up a story about her great-grandfather, right to Jane's face."

Sara's mouth opened in disbelief. She'd never even met Jane Landi. Someone else was already trying to top that lie with another, but Sara only caught part of it. She was too pissed off.

She moved out of the line to see if she recognized the gossipers.

An old friend of her nonna's, Mrs. Turati, saw her. For a moment, they stared at each other, then the woman, who had to be in her seventies, said, "How can you do this to your own neighbors, eh?"

Everyone froze, including Sara.

"Your parents are good people. Didn't they raise you better than to make up stories?"

Anger lit a bonfire in her gut. They could say whatever they wanted about her, but to malign her parents? "At least they taught me not to spread malicious rumors. But I guess your parents didn't teach you that lesson."

The whole bakery became so quiet all she could hear was the pounding of her own heartbeat. Surrounded by horrified people—some she didn't know—she inhaled her first breath since her outburst. The realization of what she'd done hit home.

Of course everyone was horrified. Once again, her quick temper was going to cost her dearly. "My parents did raise me well, and I'm sorry I said what I did. I have a great deal of love and respect for this community, which is why I decided to write about it in the first place."

Everyone stared back with sour faces.

"But I don't like to hear ugly things that aren't true being spread. This is our collective history, and I would never make up a single word about it. Regardless, I apologize. I should never have spoken to you like that. I hope, though, that the next time someone says something horrible about me or my work, you'll take a moment to ask me if it's true."

Even knowing her face was red, that leaving this way might make her a coward, she couldn't stay another minute. She didn't run, though she wanted to.

As soon as she was far enough away, she ducked into a dark entryway and called Dom.

"Sara. What's up? You okay?" The sound of hammers made it difficult to hear him.

"Oh, God." How had she forgotten? "You're working. It's not important. I'll talk to you later."

"Wait, just give me a sec."

She waited, calmer now, after hearing his voice.

"What happened?" he asked more clearly.

"It's just, everything went sideways. At my first interview, when I mentioned that their great-uncle wasn't a victim of the Black Hand, but that he'd been arrested for extortion—which I got from police records—the people freaked out as if I was accusing them of being in the Mafia or something. After that I had three cancellations in a row."

"Oh, shit. I'm so sorry."

She sniffed, trying not to let the burn behind her eyes turn into tears. "I went to Ferrara's and overheard a blatant lie about me making things up. Then one of the old goats had the nerve to say my parents raised me wrong."

"Damn. I can understand why you're so upset. Listen, I can—"

"No, no. Some of it's my fault. I shot my mouth off at Mrs. Turati, and she's old, you know, late seventies, and that scandalized everyone in the bakery."

"Where are you now?"

"About a block away from Ferrara's, on Grand."

"You know where the Mulberry Street Bar is?"

"Yeah."

"Go have a drink. I'll be there as soon as I can."

"But you're in the middle of—"

"Tony can handle it. Please, just go. It won't take me long to get there."

One tear broke through and she whisked it away. "Thank you," she said, trying not to choke from the lump in her throat.

SHE'D ONLY HAD one sip of Bushmills when Dom walked inside the crowded café bar. Dressed in faded jeans, a tight white T-shirt and work boots, his hair disheveled, he looked ridiculously hot. Sara wasn't the only woman eyeing him either. Only Dom could look that sexy in dusty work clothes.

He stretched over the small table to kiss her, then sat across from her. "Talk to me."

"I'm going to ruin everything. Again. It's my temper. I know better than to shoot off my mouth without thinking."

"Hey, someone talks crap about my parents, I'm going to give them a wake-up call, too. Did you slap her? Challenge her to a duel?"

Sara was in no mood, but that made her smile. "No. I apologized."

"That's it?"

Shaking her head, she wrapped both hands around her glass. "I told her the rumor was a lie, that if she heard anything like that again, she should check with me before she started spreading it around."

"I bet she loved that."

"I didn't stick around to see."

"Good. Don't listen to those crazy old women. All they know how to do is gossip. You can't let that crap stop you. Blasting the faculty with the truth didn't get you in trouble in school, right?"

She thought about that for a second. "I got a few slaps on the wrist, but I also got encouragement. My English teacher told me I had a bright future in journalism."

"See? And that's exactly why you're going to kick ass with this thesis. You know it's going to be great when people get pissed. That's the thing to remember. God, when you talk about the Black Hand, your eyes light up. You're still the firebrand who got us better vending machines. That dispensed condoms."

She nearly choked. "I did not ask—"

Shaking her head at his teasing grin, she laughed.

It faded when she realized just how Dom was looking at her. His gaze had darkened with admiration and respect and—dare she say, well, fondness for sure. Her chest tightened. He was her own personal champion. She'd never had that before. Not with someone she cared for so much. "You're right. I'm not going to let this go."

"That's my girl. You've been away for a while but nothing's changed. These women, this whole crazy neighborhood loves nothing better than to stir up trouble. There are going to be lots of people who realize the past is just the past, and it doesn't reflect on them personally. Like my parents, for example. Who are very excited to talk to you. And so is Nonna. She may be old, but she can remember her childhood down to what she wore to church."

The bravado that had just straightened her spine left with a whimper. If Dom knew what she did about Valente Paladino, would he be this supportive? Or would he and his family kick her to the curb?

Well, she could always leave out that part, right?

Right?

19

SARA SAT AT the Paladinos' dining room table, confident with the decision she'd made sometime in the middle of the night as she'd tossed and turned. For her own peace of mind, she'd decided to leave out Valente's name. Not even bring him up. After all, there was no way she would uncover every man who'd been associated with the Black Hand. It wasn't as if she was planning to include the whole list of them in her thesis. So choosing to leave out one name didn't make her a shitty reporter.

With that in mind, she hadn't even mentioned Valente to Dom. No reason to tell him. Although she had to wonder if that was why her stomach couldn't quite settle.

"So, time for dessert, huh?" Joe said as he returned from changing a record. More old-fashioned music drifted in from the spacious living room. "I'm not talking about fruit either."

Theresa snorted. "You keep praying to St. Jude," she said.

Sara and Dom exchanged smiles.

The single-family home was much bigger than where she'd grown up, but it had the same comfortable feel. Everything around her said family, from the pictures on the wall, the songs of Frank Sinatra and Dean Martin to the three-course meal complete with two nice Italian wines. It was almost a little too cozy, making her imagination turn to things that couldn't be. Like a home with Dom.

The foolish thought startled her. Well, no more mystery about why her stomach was wonky. She shook off the crazy idea as ruthlessly as she'd made her decision last night. The second Sara put her fork down, Theresa stood.

"I'll be right back," she said, picking up the dish of leftover ravioli and the antipasto tray.

Sara quickly pushed back, ready to help clear.

"Sit." Theresa waved her back down. "Who wants coffee?"

"We'll help later," Dom whispered. "She doesn't want us to see the dessert yet."

Sara put a hand on her tummy and smiled. "Can I help with the coffee?"

"I'll get it in a minute," Dom said, then glanced at his father, who was humming along with Sinatra. "Pop, finish telling us about Aunt Olympia."

His dad shrugged. "Not much more to tell. Until the day she passed she made most of her money as a fortune-teller. No cards, no tea leaves. She would just look at a person, close her eyes and tell them they should do this or not do that. Don't marry the skinny one. Look out for a woman with light hair—she means you harm."

Sara, who'd been delighted by Joe's memories, ached to change the subject to the Black Hand, but she'd wait till she could use the recorder. "Didn't people think she was evil? Touched by Satan?"

"Some, sure." Joe glanced briefly toward the hallway. "They wanted to have her excommunicated. But mostly the ones who didn't believe just ignored her."

"I take it Nonna didn't believe in fortune-telling," Dom said, grinning.

Sara was disappointed the woman wasn't feeling well

and hadn't joined them. But Dom was certain she'd be willing to talk when she felt better.

Mrs. Paladino returned with a cake that lit Dom's face. He got up and poured the coffee before she'd finished serving everyone a piece. Even Joe had a sliver, along with a slice of melon. He seemed pleased.

Sara was last to finish, and clearing her throat, she looked across the table. "This is by far the best walnut ricotta cake I've ever had, Mrs. Paladino. Everything was delicious."

Theresa smiled and patted the back of Sara's hand. "I'll wrap some up for you to take home."

"Thank you," Sara said, wondering if it would be rude to get her recorder. Before dinner began, Sara had asked if they'd mind if she taped their recollections, and they'd graciously agreed. But she wasn't sure if this was the right time.

"Do you like to cook, Sara? I don't mean pizza or ziti," Theresa said, shaking her head. "I like the recipe your family uses at the restaurant. The sauce is very good. Almost perfect. But Dom, he likes a little more olive oil and basil. I could teach you if you want."

Dom choked out a laugh.

"Oh, here she goes," Joe said, muttering something in Italian under his breath. "Enough, Theresa. Don't scare the girl away."

Sara didn't know quite what to say. Of course she and Dom had anticipated the whole matchmaking thing to surface. After their moms' behavior at the feast, how could they not? "Thank you, Mrs. Paladino."

"Let's talk about that later, huh, Ma?" Dom squeezed Sara's leg. "Have either of you heard stories of the Black Hand?"

Sara could have kissed him. But she hadn't missed Joe's surprised look.

"Yes, yes, I heard about those bastards." Joe glanced at her. "Excuse the language."

"That's okay," Sara said, scrambling to get her recorder on. "That's exactly how my dad described them."

Theresa looked confused. "I heard a few things, but they were more like scary monsters, not real people. My nonna would tell my brothers stories to make them behave."

Sara perked up. Interesting. Exactly the kind of tidbit she was looking for. The dilution of the facts over the years, turning it into a fairy tale. Her run of cancellations and unreturned phone calls had continued since the mess at the Di Stefanos' yesterday, and without concrete stories, her thesis would end up as bland as lukewarm tea.

"No, they were real," Joe said. "A bunch of cowards preying on their own kind. Good people who could barely feed their families."

"Why?" Theresa asked, frowning at her husband, then Dom and Sara. "What did they do to them?"

"You don't want to know," Joe said. "They were very bad men."

Sara glanced helplessly at Dom. Joe wanted to spare his wife, which Sara understood, but if he clammed up, then this was going to be a very short, useless conversation.

"I was wondering," she said. "Are you related to all the Paladinos who immigrated here in the 1890s?"

Joe nodded. "All of the Paladinos, even some who spell their names differently, are somehow related. At least the ones from Southern Italy. The three boys and I are the only ones left since my brother passed away. Francis was young, only nineteen when he died."

"Why?" Theresa asked, looking worried or suspicious. Sara wasn't sure which.

"I saw a name," Sara said, shrugging. "At the library."

"Who? What name?" Joe's expression suggested he knew who she meant.

Still, she hesitated. She could just claim to have forgotten. But Joe would know better. And probably Dom, too. "Valente Paladino," she said softly.

Joe sat back in his chair with a sigh. "What kind of document was it?"

"A police report. He was arrested for extortion."

Theresa gasped.

"Although he could very well have been a victim," Sara added quickly. "I've seen a lot of misinformation in the papers. So many people were targeted, and I've read a few accounts where innocent men ended up in prison due to false eyewitness statements."

When she glanced at Dom, she was stopped short by the shocked look on his face. She had to tell him she hadn't planned on saying anything about Valente.

"He had to be a victim," Theresa said, making it a pronouncement, not an opinion.

"I don't think so," Joe said. "I heard he was a punk kid who wanted to play the big shot. He wasn't interested in making an honest living. No one ever said exactly what he did. Just that he always had money."

"You never told me this," Theresa said. "In all these years."

Joe shrugged. "It was the worst part of my family. I didn't want you to think I was anything like him."

"Pop," Dom said. "Nobody would think that. You're the most generous guy in New York."

Joe shook his head. "I'm no saint. My family taught us to be generous. To help others. We weren't alone. How many good people do we know? Sara's parents are a perfect example. Back then people had nothing, and lived and worked in unthinkable conditions. So many were tempted by *la Mano Nera*, so who knows what really happened? Anyway, it's ancient history."

"Still." Theresa got up from the table and picked up a couple of dishes. "Do you have to mention a Paladino in your report?"

"It's not a report, Ma. It's a master's thesis, and it needs to be as accurate as possible. You remember how hard I worked on mine. I didn't want to skip any steps, and Sara shouldn't need to."

"But your papers, they were just about marketing. This is about families."

"Sara isn't doing anything wrong. In fact, she wants to give everyone a chance to tell their stories. But they're all so afraid of ruining their fairy tales."

"Well, it's *famiglia*. So you want to protect."

"Of course," Sara said. "I understand perfectly."

Dom laughed, and everyone turned to him. "Protect what? You know how the old ladies like to exaggerate and spread rumors. I doubt there's a single story that hasn't been turned inside out at one time or another."

His mother stared at him for a moment before her lashes lowered. "You're right." She walked the plates in to the kitchen, but returned to the table a moment later. "Your father's family, our family, has nothing to be ashamed of. Dominic, I'll get you another piece of cake."

DOM HADN'T STEPPED in when Sara offered to help his mother with the cleanup. Not after he'd caught his father's hint to meet him in the living room. When Dom got there, Joe was at the ancient stereo, looking through his collection of LPs.

"This research Sara's doing," Joe said, keeping his voice low. "It's fine. I know she means well, but it could lead her into some tricky areas."

"The trust."

"We've made sure to keep our names buried, but there's only so much you can hide when it comes to taxes and laws."

"I know, Pop, but I can't ask her to stop."

"No. Of course not. But, it's funny, huh? All these years, and this is the first time I've worried that things could get ugly."

"Ugly?"

"It's a long time to keep such a big secret, Dominic. People don't like to feel like they've gotten charity. You know these families. They're proud, like your mother said, and they'll think we were playing God, that we had no right."

"But—"

"They'll be mad first, and maybe then, they'll see we did it to keep our community together and safe. But just keep an eye on where she's looking, huh?"

Dom nodded, although how he was supposed to carry his task through wasn't clear. The last thing he wanted was to discourage Sara. This dissertation could be a breakthrough for her. And she deserved to have her triumph.

But he also had a huge responsibility to his family. To the years and struggles and promises generations of Paladinos had sworn to uphold and keep secret. Maybe it was for the best that he was more involved with the trust.

"There you are," Sara said, as she joined them at the stereo. He smiled, holding out his arm, wanting more than ever to support her dreams, and to keep her close.

"Oh, Dom, don't stop." Sara had her hand in his hair, trying not to pull too hard, but she didn't have much control left. The last hour had been a long, sweet seduction, from the first kiss in the elevator, to the way he'd stripped off her clothes, kissing her and licking her in places she'd never dreamed were so sensitive.

"I don't want this to end," he said, his words barely audible as he kept his lips pressed to her neck. He pulled back, achingly slowly, leaving her wanting, pushing up, locking her ankles around his hips.

His groan went straight through her, as if his voice had a direct line to her pleasure centers. "I think your voice is actually killing me."

"Oh, no, not that. Never that," he said, proving her point with his low pitch and the way he nibbled her ear as he entered her again. "You feel so good."

Hot breath wafted over her cheek, then his lips found hers, making her dizzy and needy, wanting more than she'd ever dared.

As he withdrew, he pushed up on his arms, so he could look down at her, his eyes half-closed and dark. "I can't," he whispered, as he entered her again, faster this time. Harder.

"Can't what?" Her hand moved down to his nape, hot and damp with sweat.

"Not want you." His gaze caught her, forced her to keep her own eyes open.

His rhythm changed, speeding up with each thrust.

"Don't stop," she said, meaning so much more.

The look of him, the way he stretched his head back, the tension in his body—she wanted to see this, keep her eyes open. Watch him fall apart. When it hit, his climax swept him away and shredded the last of her control. She came like a rocket, like a starburst.

When she slid back down to earth, it had all changed. Even though she knew it was impossible, that their end was inevitable, she'd fallen for Dominic.

So damn hard.

"SARA?"

"Hmm?"

Dom was curled around her, their legs entwined, his heart almost back to normal.

"Why didn't you mention Valente Paladino to me?"

"Oh, Dom, I'm so sorry," she said stiffening, and trying to move away. "I should've—"

"What you should do is stay right here," he said, holding her and stroking her back until he felt her relax a little.

"To be honest, I was hoping he wasn't related. But I'd also decided I wasn't going to use his name or bring him up at all. And then it kind of slipped. I really am sorry."

"It's okay." He had no business feeling slighted because she'd kept something from him. The weight of his own secret was heavier than he'd have imagined. There were layers between the Paladinos and the ownership records. Shell companies, mostly. The lawyers were careful, and the odds were she wouldn't find anything. But he wished he could be open with her.

Everything was different with Sara, and he wasn't sure how he'd gotten there in such a short time. He'd always held himself back, determined to keep his options wide-open. But sticking around didn't seem restrictive anymore. "I hope you know I would never ask you to leave out his name."

She nodded.

"So, how about you stay overnight?"

She ran her delicate fingers over his cheekbone. "You want that, huh?"

"To wake up to you? Yeah. I want that."

After a long, piercing look, she smiled. "I want that, too."

20

DOM SAT ALONE in Bassanova Ramen, staring at his favorite dish. The lunch crowd was noisy—the people right in back of him were slurping just loudly enough to put him on edge. He was pretty sure he'd just screwed up his third interview with *New York Adventures*.

Problem was, his mind had been a mess in the week since the dinner with his folks. He worried that Sara might uncover something that would require him to step in, which he couldn't imagine himself doing. And he worried about disappointing his family.

On the one hand, he loved seeing her in her true element. The research brought her alive. She'd even discovered a number of people, mostly those who'd already left the Lower East Side, willing to talk to her about the Black Hand. Some wanted their names changed, some wanted their names spelled correctly and a few lonely souls just wanted someone to talk to.

But on the other hand—

His cell rang with his father's tone. "Hey, give me two minutes. I can't hear you where I am."

"Call me back," Joe said.

After Dom paid for his to-go meal and left the restaurant, he walked the few blocks to Columbus Park and found a relatively quiet spot.

His father answered immediately. "Did you talk to the lawyer?"

"Yeah. He's working on it, but it's even more complicated than I thought. It's going to take some time to separate the trust and retain the rental agreements. Your will needs some alterations, too. The foundation paperwork still has to be ironed out. He's meeting with Max to talk about what the change is going to do to our taxes." Dom paused. Max had been their accountant for years. But he was getting up there and Dom didn't share his dad's confidence in the man. Better save that for later. "Anyway, we also have to talk about what to do with the management company and their contract."

"In the meantime?"

Dom rubbed his neck. He figured this call was more about what was happening with Sara. "So far so good, Sara's been concentrating on the Black Hand and hasn't stumbled onto anything that could hurt us." Yet. "I've either seen her or talked to her every night. I'll keep tabs but I think we might be worried for nothing."

"I trust you'll steer her in the right direction. Anyway, your mother's calling. I'll talk to you soon."

"Okay, Pop." After he hung up, he dialed Sara.

"Hi," she said, as if she'd just finished a run. "Are you at lunch?"

"You sound busy."

"It's packed in here. Are you still planning on meeting me at the library tonight?"

"Yeah."

"Great. I might be a few minutes late. Sorry, I've got to scramble."

They disconnected and he just sat there watching his

food get colder. And wishing he could shake the feeling this whole thing was going to turn into a big mess.

SARA BLEW INTO the research room, already slinging off her overstuffed backpack while grinning at Dom. He stood, grabbing the pack and helping her unload the notebooks he knew she'd need for this evening. The plan was to work until closing, then go back to his place. Now, all he had to do was calm himself down, starting with a kiss.

It helped.

When they finally sat, she asked, "How did your interview go?"

"Not sure," he said. "The guy in charge of marketing kept asking me about my experience with events, but the woman from PR kept reminding him of all the public speaking I've done. Maybe a wash?"

"Better than getting kicked out the door."

"That's true. You sounded like you were having a hell of a day."

Someone from a few tables away gave them a wicked "Quiet," and they both winced.

"I've been crazy busy," Sara said, her voice much lower, "but I also discovered something mighty interesting." She grabbed her notebook and flipped through a bunch of pages. "Something odd happened around 1916. There's a report in one of the smaller papers that said that some of the tenements that had made improvements based on the New Tenement Act of 1901 were charging less than some of the buildings that hadn't been redone. They all seemed to be centered around the Little Italy area. I wondered if that was some kind of deal, you know, with the Black Hand. Maybe those people who cooperated, or paid the extra money to them, somehow got lower rents."

Dom's pulse had started racing after mention of the

Tenement House Act—1916 was when the trust was first started, and those low rents were absolutely connected to the Paladino family.

"But tracing ownership to any of these buildings before 1936 is a quagmire. Lots of hiding behind company names that didn't seem to exist. Anyway, it wasn't the state setting these low rents, but that's all I could confirm."

"That's actually getting into some dangerous territory," he said. "I'm sure you know how no one likes talking about rent prices."

"Yeah. It's a forbidden topic, right up there with incest or rooting for the Yankees."

He smiled, although he wasn't finding anything amusing at the moment. "I know it probably goes against the grain, but I can't help thinking digging into this could be really tricky. Can you imagine what would happen if something you brought to light caused a bunch of rent hikes?"

SARA SAT BACK, thinking about what he'd said. The only reason Moretti's was still in business was because of the lower rent. The same went for her parents' house. Dom wasn't kidding. Stirring the pot about that could be really bad.

The crux of the matter was whether or not the information was crucial to revealing the truth about the Black Hand. She had no idea if the two things were connected. "You're right," she said. "It's tricky. And it could be that the rents don't have anything to do with anything. But I do want to find out what I can. I'll just have to be careful where I look, and who I mention it to. Obviously, I trust you not to say anything."

Dom nodded, but she could see he wasn't pleased with her solution. "Tell you what," he said. "Why don't you let me look into that? We'll keep your name out of it since you don't need any more black marks against you."

"But—but you don't have time."

"Neither do you."

Every time she thought he couldn't be any more amazing, he did or said something like this. Sara leaned close to him and pulled his hand into hers. "I can't even tell you how much your support means to me. You've been wonderful, and I know you don't have the time to spare. You must be waking up at the crack of dawn to get everything done. But every minute you're with me has been a boost to my confidence, not to mention the fact that you make me just plain happy. Please don't think I'm not taking your advice seriously. I am. I'll be careful."

She kissed him and couldn't help noticing a slight hesitancy. Maybe she needed to think about his offer some more. She trusted him. And she knew he only had her best interest at heart.

After the library closed, they stopped at the neighborhood market so he could pick up some things he needed. They'd talked and talked, not about her work, but about Ellie's ongoing search for a prom dress. She'd been asked out by a very good-looking boy and it seemed that her attention had shifted away from Dom.

As they left the store, Mrs. Masucci, a woman who lived at the edge of Little Italy, and a notorious gossip, stepped right in front of Sara.

"Don't think we all don't know what you're trying to do Sarafina Moretti. You think you can get away with tearing our families to shreds by telling your lies? You think we can't see you trying to make us look like thieves? Just because we're Italian doesn't make us the Mafia, and you're shaming yourself, your family and the whole community."

The woman looked as if she was going to spit, and Sara took a step back, stunned by the vicious attack.

Dom, however, stepped right into the old woman's face. "What the hell do you know about anything she's doing? All you live for is your gossip without any thought to who you're hurting. You did it to Catherine and now you're after Sara. If I hear one more lie coming from you, I'm going to call my attorney and we'll see how your rumors stand up in court. Do I make myself clear?"

Mrs. Masucci looked as though she might actually die on the spot. Sara was tempted to dash behind her in case she fainted, but she was too busy being stunned by Dom's fierce defense.

"Madre di Dio," Mrs. Masucci said, her voice wavering. But she wasn't looking at Dom. "You. You *strega*. You *witch*. You've turned him into a monster with your talk and your curses." She lifted a wrinkled hand, holding up her index and pinky fingers—the *mano-cummta*—to ward off curses. Then, without turning her back, she scurried past them, muttering the Rosary.

Sara burst out laughing. "What the hell just happened?"

Dom didn't join in on the hilarity. "Shit. I may have just made things worse for you."

"Hey," she said, rubbing his arm. "At least it was you this time, instead of me. Don't worry about it. She's a wicked gossip who was already lying about me. This won't make it any worse."

He started walking again, only this time to the curb to flag down a cab. Apparently he wasn't in the mood for a long stroll anymore. The look on his face silenced her.

"Dom," she said, once they were in the quiet of the taxi, "if you think it would be better to keep your distance from me, I'll understand. You have a lot going on now, and I'd hate myself if any part of this hurt you or your family."

His gentle smile eased her. "Don't be ridiculous. Although I'll do my best not to look like I've been cursed—" he leaned in close "—I can't promise I won't seem bewitched."

HE WAS BONE WEARY, and he really needed to rest. Especially after the way they'd made love. Being curled around Sara usually made him calm like nothing else. Not tonight. She was going to find out about the trust; he just knew it. And when she did, he had no idea what he would do about it. If he asked her to back off, he'd never be able to look himself in the mirror again.

"I'LL HAVE THE apple pie."

Dom grabbed the menu from his father's hand. "No he won't. You want Ma to kill me? He'll have the fresh fruit."

Joe let his head drop to his hand. "My own son. After all I've done for you."

Dom ignored him. "I'll have the same." He'd really wanted a piece of cheesecake, but he'd live.

The grinning waitress walked away, and Joe looked up. "So tell her."

It wasn't what Dom had expected to hear. "Tell Sara? Just like that?"

"You feel something for her, yes?"

Dom nodded.

"You trust her?"

"Implicitly"

"You have my blessing. Tell her."

Dom wished it was that simple, but it wasn't. And he couldn't explain without worrying the family. "Thanks, Pop. I mean it. But I'm going to wait a little longer."

"All right."

The fruit came quickly and they ate in silence, but

Dom's mind was working at a furious pace. He couldn't tell her. Once he did, he'd have to ask her to bury the information. It wouldn't be like her not naming Valente. And that was nothing compared to what might be seen as the family's behind-the-scenes manipulation. His father was right. The why behind the trust wouldn't matter. The revelation would be like lighting a bonfire in the town square.

He just wished that all this hadn't happened right after he'd taken over so much responsibility. If it all fell apart on his watch, he'd never forgive himself.

SARA KNEW DOM didn't want to talk about her work tonight. He'd made it very clear when he'd asked her to put everything away, and just be with him. And he'd been right. They'd had a wonderful evening so far. They'd actually gone to see a movie. In a theater. Shocking.

"We should do that more often," Dom said.

"I agree. Let's make a plan, say five months from now, when we both have another free night?"

He laughed, and it was nice because he hadn't been doing that much lately. Ever since he'd lashed out at Mrs. Masucci, he'd seemed different, kind of sad, but Sara hesitated to bring it up.

Maybe he was worried that *New York Adventures* hadn't gotten back to him. But it really hadn't been that long. The more she got to know him, the clearer it became that he was an extremely thoughtful man. He took his time, let things simmer. But he also didn't tend to hide things, even when she might not be happy to hear what he had to say. He would tell her what was bothering him in his own time, and together they'd make things better.

Back at his place, they didn't go straight to the bedroom. He fixed them each a drink. He'd picked up a great Irish whiskey for her, while he had red wine. Relaxing in the beautiful living room, cozy against each other, looking out his windows, the mood felt peaceful. It helped that the view was fascinating. SoHo had become a magnet for new money and tourists, but the native New Yorkers hadn't given up yet. She could see them walking their little dogs in their upscale finery.

When Dom squeezed her hand, she turned to find him smiling. "Oh," she said, "I meant to tell you yesterday. You'll never guess what I discovered. So there's this management company that handles about a third of the rentals in what used to be all of Little Italy. But the name rang a bell— What's wrong?"

His smile had vanished and his brows lowered. "Nothing."

"Oh, I forgot I'm not supposed to talk about work. Sorry."

"Go on."

"No, it's okay."

"Sara, just say it." His tone startled her.

She cleared her throat. "When I looked back at my early research, I found out they've been renting out the neighborhood since the 1900s. That's all."

His eyes closed and she watched his jaw muscles flex. When he looked at her, it was a different Dom.

"What is it about this rent thing? Why do you have to make such a big deal out of every little detail? For fuck's sake, none of this is going to change the world. This isn't some big exposé that's going to win you a Pulitzer Prize. It's a thesis. The only person who's going to give a damn about it is your professor. Oh, and the people who are nervous their rent might go up."

It was like being slapped. Worse.

He'd never used that tone or said one bad thing to her. But this? Was that what he really thought about her work?

While encouraging her, telling her that he was glad to see the fire inside her?

Yeah, well, thanks for the pat on the head.

Trembling, her heart pounding away, she had no idea what to do. Maybe being associated with the neighborhood pariah was getting to him. No, the hell with that. She wasn't about to make excuses for him.

She stood and put her drink down.

"Wait," he said, pushing himself off the couch. "Jesus. I'm sorry. I didn't mean any of that. I don't know what got into me."

"No, you're right. Nobody cares about the Black Hand… or Little Italy, for that matter. None of this stuff has any significance anymore."

"Sara, please."

She grabbed her bag and sweater. "Guess it's time for me to get over myself and quit wasting both our time."

"I don't blame you for being angry. But please—"

Screw him. She didn't care what he thought.

She rushed to the elevator and pressed the button. He came after her, but he wasn't exactly running.

21

Two hours later, Dom ended up at the gym. He'd wanted to go after Sara, but he didn't trust himself, not yet. He'd almost taken it out on the walls in the apartment, but the place belonged to his brother, and he didn't want to have to make another apology.

Pulling on a pair of gloves, he left the locker room and went straight to the heavy bags. As he pounded the damn thing, all he could think about were the nasty things he'd said to Sara, how he'd crushed her spirit. Again. Broken her heart.

He was such an asshole.

All to protect the trust. Trying to save an ungrateful community. The goddamn thing had been nothing but an albatross around every Paladino's neck. And now Sara was paying a price, as well.

His fist connected with the bag. He was feeling it in his muscles now, in his back, his thighs, his chest, but he wasn't close to being done.

Except this hole he'd dug wasn't about the trust.

The look on Sara's face would haunt him forever.

Jesus, Mr. Charming himself had handled it completely wrong. God forbid he failed at anything. Or let a single flaw show. What a selfish child he'd been. A selfish teen-ager. A selfish man.

This was his crossroads. No black or white answer. No one was going to walk out of this situation happy. Least of all him.

Panting, he let his hands drop to his sides. This would tell him what kind of a man he truly was. If he threw the problem back on his father? He'd be a coward. A quitter. But if he told Sara the truth about the trust, and asked her to squash it after promising her he'd never do that, he'd be worse than a liar.

So what was it going to be?

He had to figure out a way that only he would get the brunt of the fallout. If he could do that, maybe he'd be able to look himself in the mirror. And there was no way in hell he was going to let Sara think she was anything less then the amazing woman she was.

THE LIBRARY FELT EMPTY. Even with all the people she'd come to recognize who haunted the research rooms. Because Dom wasn't sitting across from her. Or next to her, helping her go through the massive amount of records.

Everyone at work had noticed she was depressed, no matter how hard she'd tried to fake it. Even Ellie had tried to convince her to talk to Dom.

Of course, Ellie didn't know what he'd said. Didn't know he'd called twice but Sara hadn't answered.

Thoughts of how easy it had been for Robert to manipulate her kept her from sleeping. They'd spun into perfectly logical realizations of how Dominic had spotted her weakness and jumped on the bandwagon. Or maybe he'd just felt guilty about the past.

She'd thought he'd been too good to be true. But had

she trusted her instincts? Of course not. She'd been so flattered that Dom could want her.

Squeezing her eyes shut, she promised herself she'd get off this nightmare of a merry-go-round and fall back into her work. It might not be world changing, but dammit, there was still a story to be told. The truth was what she'd been after. The truth was what she would tell. No matter what anyone else thought.

Halfway through bank records from the early 1900s, she thought about calling him.

Dammit.

Just, he'd lost his temper, and she knew that wasn't like him. Something had to be eating at him. If anyone understood how much damage losing one's temper could do…

She went back to the records. It wasn't easy keeping her focus on the work, but every time she had an errant thought, she'd pull herself back.

Discipline had never been an issue. When she set her mind to a project, she was like a dog with a bone.

A name stopped her. It wasn't even an Italian name, but it rang a bell. She'd seen it before. After saving the PDF on her rapidly filling flash drive, she went back to her notebooks, and sure enough, she found it. The maiden name of a woman who had married a Paladino back in 1918.

Turning back to the computer, she read every word on the document. A huge sum of money had been deposited into her account. Enough to send up a red flag. But according to the affidavits Sara found, there had been no improprieties. Actually, that was during the war, and while some people had removed every cent they had from anything to do with the government or banks, others had done just the opposite.

She continued her search on Mrs. Paladino née James. It wasn't easy, but as she kept digging, there were names, amounts, bank authorities, business holdings. All of them meant something, but she couldn't quite put it all together.

What she knew for sure was that the Paladinos were involved. Somehow.

Was this what had Dom so worried he'd lost control? Had more of the Paladinos been in bed with the Black Hand? Was that how they'd paid for their construction business? The house they lived in? Tony's fantastic apartment—what person who wasn't a multimillionaire could afford a whole floor in SoHo?

But what didn't make sense were the records of the management company that had actually kept rents lower, outside of the government-mandated rent control.

Certainly, her parents weren't paying off anyone to guarantee their rents. It was crazy to think Dom's parents were doing anything unethical. What was the deal here?

DOM WAS STILL a wreck, and the worst part about it was that Sara wouldn't talk to him. There was nothing left do to but force the issue. He was going to tell her about the trust. What he wasn't going to do was ask her to keep it quiet. Terrifying yes, but bottom line? He trusted Sara to do the right thing. Now all he had to do was convince her to trust him.

He waited half a block away from Moretti's, until it was ten minutes to closing. Then he made his move. Carlo was in the back and there was still a couple at a table. But Sara had the floor.

When she saw him, she was behind the counter. She froze, a wad of bills in her hand, the cash register open. "We're closing."

"I know."

"There are no slices available."

"I'm not here for a slice."

"Then I can't help you." She started counting again, but it was easy to tell she wasn't doing a great job of it.

"Sara, all I'm asking for is ten minutes. There are things to say, and I'd like to say them before we keep speeding down this road. After you know the facts, if you want me to leave, I'm gone."

"I have to close out."

He nodded and went to sit at the closest table. He pulled out his cell phone and started reading the first thing that popped up on Reddit so he wouldn't make her feel uncomfortable.

Time slowed to a trickle, and he couldn't remember one word he'd read.

Finally, the place was empty. Carlo nodded at him as he left, and he hadn't even put up the chairs. Sara came to the table with two sodas and put one down in front of Dom. "Okay," she said.

"My family has been very connected to this neighborhood for five generations. But not in the way you're thinking."

"No Black Hand?"

"Just the one. But he was a doozy. He hurt a lot of innocent people, and the rest of the family were hardworking, good folks. Avid churchgoers, gave to the poor. All they knew was that they wanted desperately to make it in America, and they wanted to do it with honor.

"One of my relatives was a skilled mason and he got into construction. But his real skill turned out to be money management. And when he'd amassed enough to make sure his family was taken care of, he started buying real estate. Not that long after, he created a trust meant to help—"

"Wait," Sara said, holding up her hand. "Of course. *A trust*. Oh, my God. That makes so much sense. That's why it was his wife who put the money in the bank. So he wouldn't be connected…"

He nodded, somehow not surprised that she'd gone on investigating and had put so much of the puzzle together. "It was a way to keep Little Italy from splintering. The low rents were strictly for the old-timers and their families to hold on to their homes and businesses. As long as the family stays in the properties, the rents are kept low. Lots of people have moved away. And when they do, we rent at the going rates."

"Wait, how many people... No, wait, that's not what I... How much is this trust worth?"

He couldn't help but laugh. "One hell of a lot."

"Is the money tied up so you can't get at it?"

"No. We can. The money isn't the issue," he said, watching her closely. "It's about privacy."

"You're not supposed to be telling me all this."

He shook his head, barely able to breathe.

Sara leaned back, letting out a long slow stream of air. "Holy shit, Dom.

"I still don't get why you all work like crazy people. Why don't you have yachts and penthouses?"

"Do we look like yacht people to you?" He hated that he couldn't read her. "Guess money doesn't stop a guy from being an asshole, huh?"

"Guess not."

"I'm still mortified at what I said to you." Flashing back to that night felt like taking a blow to the gut. "I can't apologize enough. None of it was true. I was—"

"You were scared."

He opened his mouth to argue, then nodded. "I was terrified. You're good. Working alongside you I saw how thorough and persistent you are. I knew you'd find something."

She blinked. "So, you were spying on me."

"I wouldn't call it— Yeah, I was."

"Your dad?"

Dom nodded. He wasn't about to hide anything now. Even though she didn't look too happy.

"I understand." She stared briefly at her hands. "Do you have anything else to tell me?"

"I don't know. I mean, I'll answer any questions you have."

"Actually, I figured you might have a question for me."

He finally got it. "I'm not going to ask you to bury the information."

Sara shrugged and lowered her eyes for a moment. "Hmm. I guess I'm not the best investigative journalist in the world."

"What? Don't say that."

"Dom, I'm not going to include anything about the trust in my thesis. It's not worth it. And if that makes me a lousy journalist, that's okay." She leaned closer. "It's better than being a shitty human being. Even though this stupid, ungrateful community doesn't deserve it, your family has done a lot. I'm not about to undo everything your trust has accomplished just to show everyone I'm right."

He couldn't stand it another second. He took hold of her and nearly broke his knees leaning over the table until he could reach her lips. He'd missed kissing her so much. Being without her was like losing a limb.

When they finally took a breath, she had a puzzled look on her gorgeous face.

"Go on. Ask."

"You took an awfully big chance telling me."

"Not really. The more I thought about it, the more I realized you would make the right decision. Not because you're not a great journalist, but because you and me, we care about the same things. Family. Integrity. Little Italy, whatever's left of it. And, well, I, for one, hoped like hell you cared about me."

Being far smarter than him, Sara got up, walked around the table and made him stand up. The kiss was much better. And longer. So he could hold on to what he'd gotten back.

For the second time in his life, Sara Moretti had given him another chance. One he was not going to blow.

"Okay," he said, pulling back reluctantly. "A couple of things you still need to know. First, the trust is turning into a foundation. We're going to use some of the assets to make improvements here in the community."

"Okay, sounds wonderful."

"The family agreed it's the right thing to do. They all also agreed, which is kind of nuts, but I'm going to run the foundation."

"Wow. So no *New York Adventures*?"

"Nope. But I'm going to need some help. A lot of charities are going to come knocking once the foundation is established. It won't be easy sifting through them all, trying to figure out who could use the funds most."

"I see your point."

"I'm going to need assistance, someone who's thorough and likes digging deep. So if you know of anyone…"

She lifted a brow at him, and he smiled. "There's one last thing I need to tell you. Well, to ask you."

"Okay?"

Dom looked into her beautiful eyes. What he found there was more than trust and kindness. He saw the courage he needed to take this next step. "I love you, Sara Moretti, with all my heart. Will you marry me?"

Her eyes grew large as her jaw dropped. "Are you kidding?"

"Why would I joke about something like that?"

"Well, okay then."

"Okay, what?"

She shook her head, as if he was being particularly slow. "Okay, yes. I'll marry you. And you'll marry me."

"Thank God," he whispered, pulling her tight against him. When he finally released his hold, she looked up at him.

"Our mothers are going to be complete nightmares."

His groan was cut off by a stunning kiss from the woman he loved.

Four months later...

THE FAMILY DINNERS at Joe and Theresa's had become one of Sara's favorite things. Tonight was even more special. After much searching and talking, she and Dom had finally found their dream home—a brownstone on Prince St.

Smiling at her with an excitement that felt brand new, Dom returned from the dining room with her glass of Prosecco. "Sorry about the wait. My father decided to remind me again that we should get a move on with the wedding and babies. Not that he's obsessed or anything."

He joined Sara on the couch, sitting so close they touched from shoulder to knee. Just how Sara liked it. "At least he's consistent," she said, grinning.

"You'd think it would be enough for him that Catherine's three months along, and there's Luca and April's wedding in a few months."

"I think he'll feel better when we pick a date."

"To be honest, me, too."

Sara smiled. "You'd be happy with a quick trip to city hall, when we both know the whole neighborhood would rise up in protest. But you're right. We should start narrowing things down."

He took her hand in his and threaded her fingers between his. Leaning closer, he kissed her gently. "Have I told you today how much I love you?"

"The minute we woke up, if I recall correctly."

Before he could respond, Tony showed up in front of the couch, dragging an ottoman behind him. "Hey, so, you guys talk any more about the townhouse reno? You need to get with Luca on the designs sooner rather than later. It looks like we're going to win the bid on the Green Street Hotel renovation."

Somehow, even over the sound of Dean Martin coming from the old stereo, Luca must have heard Tony, because he wandered out of the dining room with April, and joined them. "I've been doing some quick sketches on the Arts & Crafts style you were talking about. It's a great choice for that house."

"I was thinking," Sara said. "Would it be possible to make the front windows larger? The size of Tony's?"

Luca and Tony both nodded and Dom squeezed her hand. "That's a great idea, honey."

She sipped her sparkling wine, wanting to pinch herself as she listened to the brothers get all technical about what would become her new home. She'd never imagined herself with a life like this. With a future so startlingly bright.

To live in a house she'd share with the love of her life. Where, hopefully, they'd have three kids. Okay, maybe four. Where she would work as a freelance journalist, and watch her husband shine as he helped their community become a safe haven and a place of pride for the old timers as well as the new generations to come.

Soon enough, her father and Joe wandered in and added their two cents about the brownstone while Catherine and April slipped away, probably to help out Theresa and Nonna in the kitchen, along with Sara's mom. Ellie and her boyfriend were due any minute, and then the picture would be complete. Three generations together. Cooking and talking and arguing and laughing. She was the luckiest woman in all of New York. Ever since Dom had walked back into her life.

This was her family now. And she couldn't wait to see each new chapter unfold. Little Italy might be dwindling, but the spirit would never die. Not when the Paladinos were still around.

* * * * *

COMING NEXT MONTH FROM

HARLEQUIN

Blaze

Available April 18, 2017

#939 UP IN FLAMES
by Kira Sinclair
Photographer Lola Whittaker didn't intend to rekindle the flames between her and sexy smoke jumper Erik McKnight—she just climbed into the wrong bunk. And now she's pregnant!

#940 PLAYING DIRTY
by Taryn Leigh Taylor
Hockey star Cooper Mead won't let anything stop him from finally leading the Portland Storm to championship victory...but sexy, smart-mouthed bartender Lainey Harper is turning into one hell of a distraction...

#941 TEMPTING KATE
Wild Wedding Nights • by Jennifer Snow
Wedding planner Kate Hartley needs a big win to save her business, so why is the groom's brother, sexy resort owner Scott Dillon, trying to stop the wedding of the century?

#942 BEYOND THE LIMITS
Space Cowboys • by Katherine Garbera
Going to space has been astronaut Antonio Curzon's dream forever, and nothing—not even oh-so-tempting teammate and competitor Isabelle Wolsten—will stand in his way.

YOU CAN FIND MORE INFORMATION ON UPCOMING HARLEQUIN® TITLES, FREE EXCERPTS AND MORE AT WWW.HARLEQUIN.COM.

HBCNM0417

Get 2 Free Books,
Plus 2 Free Gifts—
just for trying the Reader Service!

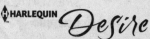 HARLEQUIN Desire

SPECIAL EXCERPT FROM

H HARLEQUIN

Blaze

*There's no way Lola Whittaker is going to rekindle the
flames between her and sexy smoke jumper
Erik McKnight—she still hasn't forgiven him for the past.*

*Read on for a sneak preview of
UP IN FLAMES,
the newest Kira Sinclair title from Harlequin Blaze!*

"Lola. It's good to see you."

"Erik. I can't say the same."

That wasn't strictly true. Because even as anger—
anger she'd been harboring for the last six years—burst
through her, she couldn't stop her gaze from rippling
down his body.

He was bigger—pure muscle. Considering the work he
did now, that was no surprise. Smoke jumping wasn't for
weaklings. It was, however, for daredevils and adrenaline
junkies. Erik McKnight was both.

Hurt flashed through his eyes. "I'm sorry you still feel
that way."

Wow, so he'd finally issued her an apology. Hardly for
the right reasons, though.

"What are you doing here?"

"Didn't your dad or Colt tell you?"

Her anger now had a new direction. The men in her
life were all oblivious morons.

"I'm—" his gaze pulled away, focusing on the sky
behind her "—taking a couple months off."

Six years ago she would have asked for an explanation.
Today she didn't want to care, so she kept her mouth shut.

"Came home to spend some time with Mom. Your dad's letting me pick up some shifts at the station."

Lola nodded. "Well, good luck with that." Hooking her thumb over her shoulder, she said, "I'm just gonna go…"

"Do anything that gets you far away from me."

She shrugged. He wasn't wrong, but her mother had raised her to be too polite to say so.

"You look good, Lola. I…I really am glad we ran into each other."

Was he serious? Lola stared at him for several seconds, searching his face before she realized that he was. Which made the anger bubbling up inside her finally burst free.

"Did you take a hit to the head, Erik? You act like I haven't been right here for the past six years, exactly where you left me when you ran away. Ran away when my brother was lying in a hospital bed, broken and bleeding."

"Because I put him there." Erik's gruff voice whispered over her.

"You're right. You did."

"That right there is why I left. I could see it every time you looked at me."

"See what?"

"Blame." His stark expression ripped through her. A small part of her wanted to reach out to him and offer comfort.

But he was right. She did blame him. For so many things.

Don't miss
UP IN FLAMES by Kira Sinclair,
available May 2017 wherever
Harlequin® Blaze® books and ebooks are sold.

www.Harlequin.com

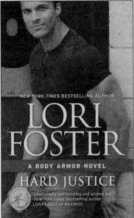